SWEEP #3

Blood Witch

Cate Tiernan

PUFFIN BOOKS

Blood Witch

Puffin Books
Published by the Penguin Group
Penguin Putnam Books for Young Readers,
345 Hudson Street, New York, New York 10014, U.S.A.
Penguin Books Ltd, 27 Wrights Lane, London W8 5TZ, England
Penguin Books Australia Ltd, Ringwood, Victoria, Australia
Penguin Books Canada Ltd, 10 Alcorn Avenue, Toronto, Ontario, Canada M4V 3B2
Penguin Books (N.Z.) Ltd, 182-190 Wairau Road, Auckland 10, New Zealand

Penguin Books Ltd, Registered Offices: Harmondsworth, Middlesex, England

Published by Puffin Books,
a division of Penguin Putnam Books for Young Readers, 2001

3 5 7 9 10 8 6 4

Produced by 17th Street Productions,
an Alloy Online, Inc. company
33 West 17th Street
New York, NY 10011

17th Street Productions and associated logos
are trademarks and/or registered trademarks of Alloy Online, Inc.

ISBN 0-14-131111-8

Printed in the United States of America

With love to my circle.

1.
Secrets

May 4, 1978

Today for the first time I helped Ma cast a circle for Belwicket. In time I'll be high priestess. Then I'll be leading the circles as she does now. Already people come to me for charms and potions, and me only seventeen! Ma says it's because I have the Riordan sight, the Riordan power, like my grandma. My own ma is a very powerful witch, stronger than anyone in Belwicket. She says I'll be stronger than that yet.

And then what, I wonder. What will I do? Make our sheep healthy? Make our fields more fertile? Heal our ponies when they go lame?

I have so many questions. Why would I have such power, the power to shake mountains? My granny's Book of Shadows says that our magick is just to be used here, in this village, this place in the country, so far away from other towns and cities. Is that so? Maybe the Goddess has a purpose for me, but I cannot see it.

— Bradhadair

For a moment the name hung in the air before me, wavering like a black insect in front of my eyes. Bradhadair! Also known as my birth mother, Maeve Riordan. I was holding her Book of Shadows, started when she first joined her mother's coven, when she was fourteen. Her Wiccan name, Bradhadair, was Gaelic for "fire starter." And I was reading words she had written in her very own hand—

"Morgan?"

I glanced up, startled. And then I felt a jolt of alarm.

My boyfriend, Cal Blaire, and his mother, Selene Belltower, stood at the entrance of the secret library. Their bodies were backlit by a shaft of light from the hall. Their faces were blank masks, hidden in shadow.

My breath caught in my throat. I had entered this room without permission. Not only had I kept Cal and our other friends waiting, I had trespassed in a private area of Selene's house. I had no business being in this room, reading these books. This I knew. A hot flush of shame made my face burn.

But I couldn't help myself. I was desperate for more knowledge—about Wicca, about my birth mother. After all, I'd only recently uncovered extraordinary secrets: that I'd been adopted, that my birth mother, a powerful witch, had been murdered, burned to death in a barn. But so many questions still remained unanswered. And now I had found Maeve Riordan's Book of Shadows: her private book of spells, thoughts, and dreams. The key to her innermost life. If the answers I sought were anywhere, they were in this book. Subconsciously—in spite of my guilt—my hands tightened around it.

"Morgan?" Cal repeated. "What are you doing in here? I've been looking all over for you."

"I'm sorry," I said, the words rushing out. I looked around, wondering how I could explain being in this place. "Uh—"

"The others went on to the movie," Cal interrupted. His voice hardened. "I told them we'd try to catch up with them, but it's too late now."

I glanced at my watch. Eight o'clock. The movie theater was at least a twenty-minute drive from here, and the movie started at eight-fifteen. I swallowed. "I'm really sorry," I said. "I just—"

"Morgan," Selene said. She stepped farther into the room. For the first time I saw tense lines on her youthful face, so like Cal's. "This is my private retreat. No one is allowed in here except me."

Now I was nervous. Her voice was calm, but I sensed the leashed anger underneath. Was I in real trouble? I stood up at her desk and closed the book. "I—I know I shouldn't be in here, and I didn't mean to intrude. But I was walking along the hall, and then suddenly I just fell against this door, and it opened. Once I was inside, I couldn't stop looking at everything. It's the most amazing library. . . ." My voice trailed off.

Selene and Cal gazed at me. I couldn't read their eyes, nor could I get any sense of what was going through their minds, and that made me even more nervous. I wasn't lying, but I hadn't told them the whole story, either. I had also been trying to avoid Sky Eventide and Hunter Niall, two English witches who were here tonight to take part in one of Selene's circles. For some reason, these two guests of Selene's filled me with inexplicable dread. When I'd heard them coming along the hall, I had tried to avoid them—and had ended up stumbling into this secret library. It had been an accident.

That's right, I thought. It *had* been an accident. Nothing

to be ashamed of. Besides, I wasn't the only one who had some explaining to do. I had a few questions for Selene.

"This is Maeve Riordan's Book of Shadows," I found myself saying. My voice sounded loud, harsh in my ears. "Why do you have it? And why didn't you tell me you had it? You both know I've been trying to find out about her. I mean . . . don't you think I'd want to see something that belonged to her?"

Cal seemed surprised. He glanced at his mother.

Selene reached behind her and shut the door, closing us all inside the secret room. No one walking down the hall would ever notice the door's almost invisible line. Her beautiful eyebrows arched as she came closer to me.

"I know you've been trying to find out about your mother," she said. In the golden halo of the lamplight her expression seemed to soften. She glanced at the book. "How much have you read?"

"Not a lot." I chewed my lip anxiously.

"Have you come across anything surprising?"

"Not really," I said, watching her.

"Well, a Book of Shadows is a very personal thing," Selene said. "Secrets are revealed there, unexpected things. I was waiting to tell you about it because I know what it contains, and I wasn't sure you were ready to read it." Her voice fell to a whisper. "I'm not sure you're ready now, but it's too late."

My face tightened. Maybe I had been violating a private area of her house, but I had a right to know about my mother. "But it's not really your decision to make," I argued. "I mean, she was *my* mother. Her Book of Shadows should be mine. That's what you're supposed to do with Books of Shadows, pass them down to your children. It *is* mine."

Selene blinked at my strong words. She glanced at Cal again, but he was looking at me. Once more my fingers tingled as they traced the book's worn leather cover.

"So why do you have it?" I repeated.

"I got it by accident," Selene said. A fleeting smile crossed her face. "Though of course most witches don't believe in accidents. My hobby is collecting Books of Shadows—really, I collect almost any book having to do with witchcraft, as you can see." She waved an elegant hand at the shelves in the room. "I work with several dealers, mostly in Europe, who have standing orders to send me whatever books they have of interest—any Book of Shadows, no matter what its condition. I find them fascinating. I take them with me wherever we go and set them up in a private study, as I did here when we moved in this past summer. To me, they're a window into the human side of the craft. They're diaries, records of experiments; they're people's histories. I have over two hundred Books of Shadows, and Maeve Riordan's is just one of them."

I waited for her to elaborate, but she didn't. Her response sounded strangely voyeuristic—especially from a high priestess, someone who was otherwise so in touch with people's feelings. Why couldn't she see that Maeve Riordan's book wasn't just another Book of Shadows? At least not to me.

My initial guilt and nervousness were giving way to anger. Selene had read my mother's private words. But right then Cal stepped across the room and put his hand on my shoulder, rubbing gently. He seemed to be saying he was on my side, that he understood. So why couldn't his mother? Did she think I was too much of a child to handle my mother's secrets?

"Where did you get *this* Book of Shadows?" I asked insistently.

"From a dealer in Manhattan," Selene said. Once again her tone was impossible to read. "He had acquired it from someone else—someone who had no credentials, who may have stolen it or found it in a second-hand store somewhere." She shrugged. "I bought it about ten or eleven years ago, sight unseen. When I opened it, I realized it was by the same young witch who I'd read about dying in a fire, not far from here. It's a special Book of Shadows, and not just because it's Maeve's."

"I'm going to take it home," I said boldly, surprising myself again.

For a long moment silence hung thick in the air. Again my heart started to race. I'd never challenged Cal's mother before; I hardly ever challenged adults at all . . . and she was a powerful witch. Cal's eyes flashed between the two of us.

"Of course, my dear," Selene finally said. "It's yours."

I let my breath out silently. Selene added, "After Cal told me your story, I knew one day I would give it to you. If, after you read it, you have any questions or concerns, I hope you'll come and talk to me."

I nodded. "Thanks," I mumbled. I turned to Cal. "You know, I really just want to go home now." My voice was shaky.

"Okay," Cal said. "I'll drive you. Let's get our coats."

Selene stepped aside to let us pass. She remained in the study, probably to look around at what else I had touched or examined. Not that I could blame her. I didn't know what to feel. I hadn't meant to abuse her trust, but there was no denying the reward: I now possessed an intimate record of my birth mother's life, written in her hand. No matter what mysteries lay inside, I knew I could handle them. I *had* to handle them.

Cal squeezed my shoulder as we walked down the hall, reassuring me.

Outside, the November wind whipped through my hair, and I brushed it out of my face. Cal opened his car and I climbed in, shivering against the cold leather seats and pushing my hands deep inside my pockets. The Book of Shadows was zipped up inside my jacket, next to my chest.

"The heater will warm things up in a minute," Cal said. He turned the key and punched buttons on the dash. His handsome face was just a silhouette in the dark of night. Then he turned to me and brushed his hand, surprisingly warm, against my cheek. "Are you okay?" he asked.

I nodded, but I wasn't sure. I was grateful for his concern, yet I was all wrapped up in the mystery of the book and still uneasy about what had just happened with Selene.

"I wasn't trying to spy or sneak around," I told him. The words were true, but they sounded even less convincing the second time around.

He glanced at me again as he turned the Explorer onto the main road. "That door is spelled shut," he said thoughtfully. "I still have to get Mom's permission to go in—I've never been able to open the door by myself. And believe me, I've tried." His grin was a white flash in the darkness.

"But that's weird," I said, frowning. "I mean, I didn't even try to open the door—it just popped open, and I almost fell down."

Cal didn't respond. He concentrated on the road. Maybe he was trying to figure out how I had gotten in there, wondering if I'd used magick. But I hadn't, at least not consciously. Maybe I had been destined to find my way into that study, to find my mother's book.

Snow had started to fall, and now it brushed against the windshield, not sticking anywhere. It would be gone by morning. I couldn't wait to get home, to run upstairs to my room and start reading. For some reason, my thoughts turned to Sky Eventide and Hunter Niall. I had instantly disliked both of them: their piercing gazes, their snotty English accents, the way they looked at Cal and at me.

But why? Who were they? Why did they seem so important? I'd only seen Sky once before, in the cemetery a few days ago. And Hunter—Hunter upset me in a way I couldn't explain. I was still thinking about it when Cal pulled into my driveway and switched off the engine.

"Are your folks home?" he asked.

I nodded.

"Are you okay? Do you want me to come in?"

"That's all right," I said, appreciating his offer. "I think I'll just hole up and read."

"Okay. Listen, I'll be home all night. Just call me if you want to talk."

"Thanks," I said, reaching for him.

He came into my arms, and we kissed for a few moments. The sweetness momentarily washed away any confusion and uncertainty I was feeling about my encounter with Selene. Finally, reluctantly, I untangled myself and opened the car door.

"Thanks," I said again. "I'll call you."

"Okay. Take care." He gave me a smile and didn't leave until I was inside.

"Hi!" I called. "I'm home."

My parents were watching a movie in the family room. "You're early," said Mom, looking at the clock.

I shrugged. "We missed the movie," I explained. "And I just decided to come home. Well, I'll be upstairs." I fled up to my room, ditched my coat, and flopped down on my bed. Then I pulled out a *Scientific American* magazine and got it ready in case I suddenly needed to cover the Book of Shadows. My parents and I had reached an uneasy truce—about Wicca, about my birth mother, about all the deception. It was best not to disturb that. I didn't want to have to explain anything painful to them.

Maeve Riordan's own words, I thought.

My hands trembling, I opened my mother's Book of Shadows and began to read.

2.
Picketts Road

What to write? The pressure inside me is building until my head pounds. Until recently I've always wanted to do what I needed to do. Now for the first time these two paths are diverging. She is blooming like an orchid: transforming from a plain plant into something crushingly beautiful, a blossom that cries out to be picked.

But now, somehow, the thought bothers me. I know it's right, it's necessary, it's expected. And I know I'll do it, but they keep hounding me. Nothing is turning out the way I had envisioned. I need more time to tie her to me, to join with her mentally, emotionally, so she'll see through my eyes. I even find myself liking the idea of joining with her. I'll bet the Goddess is laughing at me.

As to craft, I've found a variant reading of Hellorus that describes how sitting beneath an oak can bend the will of Eolh. I want to try it soon.

    —Sgàth

Saturday morning I didn't exactly leap out of bed. I'd been up until the wee hours, reading Maeve's Book of Shadows. She'd started it when she was fourteen years old. So far, I couldn't figure out what Selene meant about finding out something upsetting. Aside from unpronounceable Gaelic words and lots of spells and recipes, I hadn't found anything really disturbing or strange. I knew that Maeve Riordan and Angus Bramson, my birth parents, were burned to death after they came to America. I just didn't know why. Maybe this book would explain it somehow. But I was reading slowly. I wanted to savor every word.

When I finally woke up and groped my way downstairs, my eyes were slits. I stumbled toward the refrigerator for a Diet Coke.

I was working on a couple of Pop-Tarts when Mom and Mary K. breezed in, having taken a brisk mother-daughter walk in the chill November air.

"Wow!" said Mom, her nose pink. She clapped her gloved hands. "It's nippy outside!" She came over and gave me a kiss, and I flinched as her icy hair brushed against my face.

"It's pretty, though," Mary K. added. "The snow is just starting to melt, and all the squirrels and birds are on the ground, looking for something to eat."

I rolled my eyes. Some people are just too cheerful in the morning. It isn't natural.

"Speaking of something to eat," Mom said, taking off her gloves and sitting down across from me, "can you two hit the grocery store this morning? I'm showing a house at ten-thirty, and we're out of almost everything."

Mentally I reviewed my blank calendar. "Sure," I said. "Got a list?"

Mom plucked it off the fridge and started adding items to it. Mary K. put the last bagel in the toaster. The phone rang, and she whirled to get it.

Cal, I thought, my heart picking up a beat. Happiness washed over me.

"Hello?" answered Mary K., sounding perky and breathless at the same time. "Oh, hi. Yeah, she's here. Just a sec."

She handed the phone to me, mouthing, "Cal."

I knew it. Ever since I'd discovered Wicca, since I'd discovered Cal, I'd always been able to tell who was calling. "Hi," I said into the phone.

"How are you?" he asked. "Did you stay up all night, reading?"

He knew me. "Yes . . . I want to talk to you about it," I said. I was very aware of my mother and Mary K. sitting right there, especially since Mary K. was patting her heart and making swooning gestures at me. I frowned.

"Good—I'd like that," Cal said. "Want to drive up to Practical Magick this afternoon?"

Practical Magick was a Wicca store in the nearby town of Red Kill, and one of my favorite places to spend a spare hour or two. "I'd love to," I said. My frown melted into a smile. All my senses were waking up.

"I'll come get you. Say, one-thirty?"

"Okay. See you then."

I hung up the phone. My mom lowered the newspaper and looked at me over her reading glasses.

"What?" I said self-consciously, a big grin on my face.

"Everything going all right with Cal?" she asked.

"Uh-huh," I said. I could feel my cheeks reddening. It felt

weird to talk to my parents about my boyfriend—especially since he was the one who had introduced me to Wicca. I'd always been able to discuss my life with Mom and Dad, but Wicca was a part of it they wanted gone, forever. It had created a wall between us.

"Cal seems nice," Mom said brightly, trying to put me at ease and fish for information at the same time. "He's certainly good-looking."

"Um . . . yeah, he's really nice. Let me go take a shower," I mumbled, standing up. "Then we'll go to the store."

I fled.

"Okay, first stop, coffee shop," Mary K. directed a half hour later. She folded Mom's grocery list and stuck it in her coat pocket.

I wheeled Das Boot—my massive, submarinelike old car—into the parking lot of the small strip mall that boasted Widow's Vale's one and only coffee emporium. We dashed from the car to the café, where it smelled like coffee and pastry. I looked at the board and tried to decide between a grande latte or a grande today's special. Mary K. leaned over the glass case, gazing longingly at the bear claws. I checked my cash.

"Get one if you want," I said. "My treat. Get me one, too."

My sister flashed me a smile, and I thought again that she looked so much older than fourteen. Some fourteen-year-olds are so gawky: half formed, childlike. Mary K. wasn't. She was savvy and mature. For the first time in a long while, it occurred to me that I was lucky to have her as my sister, even if we didn't share the same blood.

The door swung open, bells jangling. Bakker Blackburn

came in, followed by his older brother, Roger, who had been a senior at Widow's Vale High last year and was now at Vassar. My insides clenched. Mary K. glanced up, eyes wide. She looked away quickly.

"Hey, Mary K., Morgan," Bakker mumbled, avoiding my gaze. He probably hated me. About a week earlier, I'd kicked him out of our house in no uncertain terms when I'd found him pinning Mary K. down on her bed, practically raping her. He also probably thought I was an alien, since those terms had included hitting him with a ball of crackly blue witch fire—without even meaning to. I still didn't know how I'd done it. My own power constantly surprised me.

Mary K. nodded at Bakker. She clearly didn't know what to say.

"Hey, Roger," I said. He was two years older than me, but Widow's Vale is a small town, and we all pretty much know each other. "How's it going?"

Roger shrugged. "Not bad."

Bakker's eyes remained glued to Mary K.

"We'd better go," I stated, heading toward the exit.

Mary K. nodded, but she took her time following me out the door. Maybe she secretly wanted to see if Bakker would say anything. Sure enough, he approached her.

"Mary K.," he began pleadingly.

She looked at him but turned and caught up to me without a word. I was relieved. I knew he'd been groveling hard since The Incident, and I could tell that Mary K. was weakening. I was afraid that if I spoke too harshly, it might drive her back to him. So I kept my mouth shut. But I had promised myself that if I got the slightest inkling of his forcing himself

on her again, I would tell my parents, his parents, and everyone I knew.

And Mary K. would probably never forgive me, I thought
as we got into the car.

I started Das Boot's engine and pulled out onto the
street. Thinking about Mary K.'s love life made me think
about my own. I started to smile and couldn't stop. Was Cal
my mùirn beatha dàn—the Wiccan term for soul mate, life
partner? He seemed to believe so. The possibility sent a
shiver down my spine.

At the grocery store we stocked up on Pop-Tarts and
other necessities. In the snacks aisle I lifted twelve-packs of
Diet Coke into the cart while Mary K. piled bags of pretzels
and chips on top. Farther down the shelf were boxes of
Fudge Therapy, Bree's favorite junk food.

Bree. My former best friend.

I swallowed. How many times had Bree and I smuggled
boxes of Fudge Therapy into a movie theater? How many
boxes had we consumed during sleep overs as we lay in the
dark, spilling our secrets to each other? It still seemed bizarre
that we were enemies, that our friendship had broken up
because she had wanted Cal and he had wanted me. In the past
few weeks I had wished again and again that I could talk to her
about all that I'd learned. Bree didn't even know I was adopted.
She still thought I was a Rowlands by birth, like Mary K. But
Bree was being such a bitch to me now, and I was being cold to
her. Oh, well. For now, there was nothing I could do about it. It
seemed best not to dwell on what I couldn't change.

Mary K. and I checked out and loaded up the car. I stifled a yawn as we climbed back in. The gray, cheerless

weather seemed to sap my energy. I wanted to go home and nap before Cal came over.

"Let's go down Picketts Road," said Mary K., adjusting the car's heater vents to blow right on her. "It's so pretty, even if it takes longer."

"Picketts Road it is," I said, taking the turn. I preferred this route, too: it was hilly and winding, and there weren't many houses. People kept horses back here, and though most of the trees were now bare, colorful leaves still littered the ground, like the patterns on an oriental carpet.

Up ahead were two cars parked by the side of the road. My eyes narrowed. I recognized them as Matt Adler's white jeep and Raven Meltzer's beat-up black Peugeot . . . parked right next to each other on a road few people used. That was odd. I hadn't even realized that they spoke to each other. I looked around but didn't see either one of them.

"Interesting," I muttered.

"What?" said my sister, fiddling with the radio dial.

"That was Matt Adler's jeep and Raven Meltzer's Peugeot," I said.

"So?"

"They're not even friends," I said, shrugging. "What are their cars doing out here?"

Mary K. pursed her lips. "Gosh, maybe they killed someone and are burying the body," she said sarcastically.

I smirked at her. "It's just kind of unusual, that's all. I mean, Matt is Jenna's boyfriend, and Raven . . ." Raven doesn't care if a guy is someone's boyfriend, I finished silently. Raven just liked to get guys, chew them up, and spit them out.

"Yeah, but they both do this Wicca stuff with you, right?"

said Mary K., flipping down the sun visor mirror to check her appearance. It was obvious that she didn't want to look me in the eye. She'd made it very clear that she disapproved of "this Wicca stuff," as she liked to call it.

"But Raven's not in our coven," I said. "She and Bree started their own coven."

"Because you and Bree aren't talking anymore?" she asked pointedly, still looking in the mirror.

I bit my lip. I still hadn't explained very much about Bree and Cal to my family. They had noticed, of course, that Bree and I weren't hanging out and that Bree wasn't calling the house nine times a day. But I'd mumbled something about Bree being busy with a new boyfriend, and no one had called me on it till now.

"That's part of it," I said with a sigh. "She thought she was in love with Cal. But he wanted to be with me. So Bree decided the hell with me." It hurt to say it out loud.

"And you chose Cal," my sister said, but her tone was forgiving.

I shook my head. "It's not like I chose Cal *over* her. Actually, she chose him over me first. Besides, I didn't tell Bree she had to get out of my life or anything. I still wanted to be friends."

Mary K. flipped the visor back up. "Even though she loved your boyfriend."

"She *thought* she loved him," I said, getting prickly. "She didn't even know him, though. She still doesn't. Anyway, you know how she is about guys. She likes the thrill of the chase and the conquest much more than any long-term thing. Use them and lose them. And Cal didn't want to be with her." I sighed again. "It's complicated."

Mary K. shrugged.

"You think I shouldn't go out with Cal just because Bree wanted him?" I asked. My knuckles whitened on the steering wheel.

"No, not exactly," said Mary K. "It's just, I feel kind of sorry for Bree. She lost you *and* Cal."

I sniffed. "Well, she's being a total bitch to me now," I muttered, forgetting how much I had been missing Bree just minutes ago. "So she obviously isn't all broken up about it."

Mary K. stared out the window. "Maybe being a bitch is just how Bree acts sad," she murmured absently, watching the barren trees pass. "If you were my best friend for about twelve years and you left me for a guy you just met, maybe I would be a bitch, too."

I didn't answer. Just stay out of it, I thought. Like my fourteen-year-old sister knew anything. She'd allowed herself to get involved with a sleazebag like Bakker, after all.

But deep down, I wondered if I was irritated because Mary K. was right.

3.
Woodbane

Litha, 1998

This is the time of year when I am most sad. Sad and angry. One of the last circles that I did with my mum and dad was for Beltane, eight years ago. I was eight, Linden was six, and Alwyn was only four. I remember the three of us sitting with the other kids, sons and daughters of the coven's members. The warmth of May was trying to steal in and banish April's cold, dreary wetness. Around our maypole the grown-ups were laughing and drinking wine. We kids danced, weaving our ribbons in and out of each other, gathering magick to us in a pastel net.

I felt the magick inside me, inside everything. I was so impatient. I didn't know how I'd ever make it till I was fourteen, when I could be initiated as a full witch. I remember the sunset glowing on Mum's hair, and she and Dad held each other, kissing, while the others laughed. The other kids and I groaned and covered our faces. But we were only pretending to be embarrassed. Inside, our spirits were dancing. The air was full of life, and everything was glowing and swelling with light and wonder and happiness.

And before Litha, seven weeks later, Mum was gone, Dad was gone—vanished, without a trace, without a word to us, their children. And my life changed forever. My spirit shriveled, shrank, twisted.

Now I'm a witch and almost full-grown. Yet inside, my spirit is still a mean, twisted thing. And even though I have since learned the truth, I am still angry—in some ways, more than I have ever been. Will it always be that way? Maybe only the Goddess knows.

—Giomanach

After lunch I was in my room, twisting my long hair into a braid, when I felt Cal's presence. A smile spread across my face. I focused my senses and felt my parents in the living room, my sister in the bathroom—and then Cal, coming closer, tickling my nerves as he approached. By the time I snapped an elastic around my braid, he was ringing the doorbell. I dashed from my room and down the stairs.

Mom answered the door.

"Hello, Cal," she said. She'd met him once before, when he'd come to visit after Bree had practically broken my nose with a volleyball during gym. I could feel her giving him the standard maternal up-and-down as he stood there.

"Hi, Mrs. Rowlands," Cal replied easily, smiling. "Is Morgan—oh, there she is." Our eyes met, and we grinned foolishly at each other. I couldn't hide the pleasure that I took in seeing him, not even from my mom.

"Will you be back for dinner?" Mom asked, unable to resist giving me a quick kiss.

"Yes," I said. "And then I'm going to Jenna's tonight."

"Okay." Mom took a deep breath, then smiled at Cal again. "Have a good time."

I knew that she was trying hard not to ask Cal to drive safely, and to her credit, she managed it. I waved good-bye and hurried out to Cal's car.

He climbed in and started the engine. "Still want to go to Practical Magick?" he asked.

"Yes." I settled back in my seat. My thoughts instantly turned to the night before, to finding Maeve's Book of Shadows.

As soon as we were out of eyesight of my house, Cal pulled the car over and reached across to kiss me. I moved as close to him as I could in the bucket seats and held him tightly. It was so strange: I had always counted on Bree and my family for grounding, for support. But now Bree was out of my life, and my family and I were still coming to terms with the fact that I was adopted. If it weren't for Cal . . . well, it seemed best not to think of that.

"Are you okay?" he asked, pulling back to kiss my face again. "No worries with the BOS?"

"Not yet," I told him, shaking my head. "It's really amazing, though. I'm learning so much." I paused. "Your mom isn't mad I took it, is she?"

"No. She knows it's yours. She should have told you about it." He smiled ruefully. "It's just—I don't know. Mom is used to being in charge, you know? She leads her coven. She's a high priestess. She's always helping people solve problems, helping them with stuff. So sometimes she acts like she's got to protect the whole world. Whether they want her to or not."

I nodded, trying to understand. "Yeah. I can see that. I guess I just felt that it wasn't really her business, you know? Or maybe it could be, but it should be my business first."

There was a flash of faint surprise in Cal's eyes, and he gave a dry laugh. "You're funny," he said. "Usually people are swarming all over my mom. Everyone is so impressed with her power, her strength. They blurt out all their problems and tell her everything, and they want to be as close to her as possible. She's not used to people challenging her."

"But I like her a lot," I said, worried that I'd sounded too harsh. "I mean, I—"

"No, it's okay," he interrupted, nodding. "It's refreshing. You want to stand on your own two feet, do things yourself. You're your own person. It makes you interesting."

I didn't know what to say. I blushed slightly.

Cal pulled my braid out from underneath my coat. "I love your hair," he murmured, watching the braid run through his fingers. "Witch hair." Then he gave me a lopsided grin and shifted the car into gear.

Now I knew my face must be bright red. But I sat back, feeling happy and strong and unsure all at once. My eyes wandered out the window as we drove. The clouds had darkened, moving sluggishly across the sky as if trying to decide when to start dumping snow. By the time we reached

Red Kill, they let loose with big, wet flakes that stuck to everything in clumps.

"Here we go," said Cal, turning on his windshield wipers. "Welcome to winter."

I smiled. Somehow the falling snow and thumping wipers made the silence inside the car even more peaceful. I was so glad to be here right now, in this moment, with Cal. I felt like I could tackle anything.

"You know, there's something I meant to tell you before," I said. "The other day I followed Bree because I wanted to have it out with her once and for all."

Cal glanced over at me. "Really?"

I nodded. "Yeah—but it didn't end up that way. Instead I saw her and Raven meeting Sky Eventide."

His hand darted away, and he shot another quick glance at me. His brow was furrowed. "Sky?"

"Yeah, the blond witch I met last night at your mom's." The really good-looking one, I thought with an odd pang of jealousy. Even though I knew Cal loved me, that he had *chosen* me, I still felt insecure, especially when we were around pretty girls. It was just that he was so handsome, with his golden eyes and tall frame and perfect body. And I . . . well, I wasn't so perfect. A flat-chested girl with a big nose could hardly be called perfect.

"Anyway, I saw Sky with Bree and Raven," I continued, shoving my insecurities aside. "I bet she's the blood witch they have in their coven."

"Hmmm," said Cal. He gazed forward at the road, as if thinking intently. "Really. Yeah, I guess it's possible."

"Is she . . . bad?" I asked, for lack of a better term. "I mean, I feel like you dislike her and Hunter, too. Are they, I don't know, from the dark side?" I stumbled over the words. They sounded so melodramatic.

Cal laughed, startled. "Dark side? You've been watching too many movies. There's no dark side to Wicca. It's just a big circle. Everything magickal is part of that circle. You, me, the world, Hunter, Sky, everything. We're all connected."

I frowned. It seemed a strange thing to say, considering the way he'd glared at Hunter and Sky. "Last night you guys seemed to not like each other," I persisted.

Cal shrugged. He turned onto Red Kill's main street and cruised slowly, looking for a parking spot. After a few moments' silence he finally said, "Sometimes you just meet people who rub you the wrong way. I met Hunter a couple of years ago, and . . . we just can't stand each other." He laughed as if it were no big deal. "Everything about him pisses me off, and it's mutual. That doesn't sound very witchy, I know. But I don't trust him."

"What do you mean? Trust him as a person or a witch?"

Cal parked the car at an angle and turned off the engine. "There isn't a difference," he muttered. His expression was distant.

"What about the big circle?" I asked, unable to help myself. "If you're connected, then how can he piss you off so much?"

"It's just . . . ," he began, then shook his head. "Forget it. Let's talk about something else." He opened his door and stepped out into snowfall.

I opened my mouth, then closed it. Pursuing the conversation seemed important. After all, Hunter and Sky had both had a profound effect on me, and I couldn't figure out why. But if Cal wanted to leave it alone, I could respect that.

There were things I didn't want to talk about with him, either. I hopped out of the car and slammed the door behind me, then ran to catch up with him.

"It's too bad you don't have anything else of your mom's," Cal remarked as we walked toward the cozy little shop. We both buried our faces in our coats to protect ourselves from the cold. "Like the coven's tools, its athame, or wand, or maybe your mom's robe. Those things would be great to have."

"Yeah," I agreed. "But I guess all that stuff's long gone by now."

Cal swung open Practical Magick's heavy glass door, and I ducked inside. Warm air wafted over us, rich with the scent of herbs. We stamped the snow off our shoes, and I took off my gloves. I smiled. Automatically I started scanning book titles on the shelves. I loved this store. I could stay here and read all day. I glanced at Cal. He was already reading book spines, too.

Alyce and David, the two store clerks, were both in the back, talking quietly to customers. My eyes immediately flashed from David—with his short gray hair, his unusually youthful face, and his piercing dark eyes—to Alyce. I'd felt a connection with Alyce the first time I had met her. It was Alyce who had told me the story of my birth mother, how her coven had been completely destroyed. From Alyce, I'd learned that Maeve and my father had fled for America and settled in Meshomah Falls, a town about two hours from here. In America they had renounced magick and witchcraft and lived quietly by themselves. Then, about seven months after I was born, they gave me up for adoption. Soon after that they had been locked in a barn, and the barn was set on fire.

"Have you read this?" Cal asked, breaking into my thoughts. He reached for a book on a shelf near the register. Its title was *Gardens of the Craft.* "My mom has a copy of it. She uses it a lot."

"Really?" I took it from him, intrigued. I hadn't remembered seeing it in Selene's library. Then again, there had been hundreds of books. "Oh, this is incredible," I murmured, flipping through the pages. It was all about laying out an herb garden to maximize its potential, to get the most out of healing plants and plants for spells. "This is exactly what I want to do—"

I broke off. At the very back of the book there was a chapter titled "Spells to Cross Foes." An unpleasant tingling sensation crept across my neck. What did that mean, exactly? Could the plants' magick be used to harm people? It didn't seem right somehow. On the other hand, maybe a witch needed to know about the negative possibilities of herbal magick—in order to guard against them. Yes. Maybe that knowledge was a crucial part of the big circle of Wicca that Cal had mentioned only moments ago.

Gently Cal took the book from me and tucked it under his arm. "I'll get it for you," he said, kissing me. "As a pre-birthday present."

I nodded, feeling my concerns evaporate in a wash of pleasure. My seventeenth birthday was still eight days away. I was surprised and thrilled that Cal was thinking about it already.

We started walking through the store. I'd never been here with Cal, and he showed me hidden treasures I'd never noticed before. First we looked at candles. Each color of candle had different properties, and Cal told me about which ones were used in which rituals. My mind whirled with all of the names. There was so much to learn. Next we examined sets of small bowls. Wiccans used them to hold salt or other ritual substances, like water or incense. Cal told me that when he lived in California, he and Selene had spent a whole summer gathering ocean water and evaporating it for the salt. They saved the salt and used it to purify their circles for almost a year afterward.

After that we saw brass bells that helped charge energy fields during a circle, and Cal pointed out magickally charged twine and thread and ink. These were everyday objects, but they had been transformed. Like me, I thought. I almost laughed aloud with pleasure. Magick was in everything, and a truly knowledgeable witch could use literally anything to imbue spells with power. I'd had glimpses of this knowledge before, but with Cal here—really showing it to me—it seemed more real, more accessible, and infinitely more exciting than it ever had before.

And everywhere there were books: on runes, on how the positions of the stars affected one's spells, on the healing uses of magic, on how to increase one's power. Cal pointed out several he thought I should read but said he had copies and would lend them to me.

"Do you have a magickal robe yet?" he suddenly asked. He gestured to one on a rack near the rear of the store. It was made of deep blue silk that flowed like water.

I shook my head.

"I think that by Imbolc we should start using robes in our circles," he said. "I'll speak to the others about it. Robes are usually better than street clothes for making magick: you wear them only when you're doing magick, so they don't get contaminated with the jangled vibrations of the rest of your life. And they're comfortable, practical."

I nodded, brushing my hand against the fabric of the different robes. The variety was astounding. Some were plain; some were painted or sewn with magickal symbols and runes. But I didn't see any that I felt I absolutely had to have, though they were all beautiful. That was okay, though; Imbolc wasn't until the end of January. I had plenty of time to find one.

"Do you wear a robe?" I asked.

"Uh-huh," he said. "Whenever I do a circle with my mom or by myself. Mine is white, a really heavy linen. I've had it a couple of years. I sort of wish I could wear it all the time," he added with a grin. "But I don't think the people of Widow's Vale are ready for that."

I laughed, picturing him casually walking into Schweickhardt's drugstore in a long, white robe.

"Sometimes robes are passed down from generation to generation," Cal continued. "Like tools. Or sometimes people weave the cloth and sew them themselves. It's like anything else—the more thought and energy you put into something, the more it stores up magickal energy and the more it can help you focus when you do spells."

I was beginning to understand that, although I knew I would spend a lot of time meditating on how I could start applying it to my own magickal doings.

Cal stepped across the aisle and reached for something on an upper shelf. It was an athame: a ceremonial dagger, about ten inches long. The blade was made of silver, so brightly polished, it looked like a mirror. Its handle was carved with silver roses. There was a skull joining the handle and the blade together.

"It's beautiful, isn't it?" Cal murmured.

"Why does it have a skull on it?" I asked.

"To remind us that in life, there is always death," he said quietly, turning it in his fingers. "There is darkness in light, there is pain in joy, and there are thorns on the rose." He sounded solemn and thoughtful, and I shivered.

Then he glanced up at me. "Maybe a certain lucky someone will get it for her birthday."

I wiggled my eyebrows, looking hopeful, and he laughed.

It was getting late, and I had to get home. Cal checked out, buying some green candles, some incense, and the book on gardening for me. I felt Alyce's eyes on me.

"Nothing for you?" she asked in her gentle way.

I shook my head.

She hesitated, then cast a quick glance at Cal. "I have something I think you should read," she said to me. Moving with surprising grace for a short, round person, she left the counter and walked down the aisle of books. I shrugged at Cal—and then Alyce was back, her lavender skirts swishing. She handed me a plain, dark brown book.

"Woodbane, Fact and Fiction," I read aloud. A chill shot through my body. The Woodbanes were the darkest of the seven ancient Wiccan clans, notorious for their quest for power at any cost. The evil ones. I looked at her, baffled. "Why should I read this?" I asked.

Alyce met my gaze squarely. "It's an interesting book that

debunks many of the myths surrounding the Woodbanes," she said, ringing it up. "It's useful for any student of the craft."

I didn't know what to say, but I pulled out my wallet and counted out money, pushing the bills across the counter. I trusted Alyce. If she thought I should read this, I would. But at the same time I was aware of tension tightening Cal's body. He wasn't angry, but he seemed hyperalert, watching Alyce, watching me, measuring everything. I put my arm around his waist and gave him a reassuring squeeze.

He smiled.

"Good-bye, Alyce," I said. "Thanks."

"My pleasure," she replied. "Good-bye, Morgan. Good-bye, Cal."

I held my two new books under my arm as we walked to the door—one book I wanted to read, one I didn't. Yet I would read them both. Although I had been studying witch-craft for barely two months, I had already learned a valuable lesson: Everything had two sides. I had to take the good with the bad, the fun with the discomfort, the excitement with the fear. The thorns with the rose.

Cal pushed open the door, and the bells jingled.

He stopped so suddenly that I walked right into his back.

"Oof," I said, steadying myself. I peeked around him.

That was when I saw what had made him pause.

It was Hunter Niall, crouched in the street, looking under Cal's car.

4.
Spell

Litha, 1990

I'm frightened. I woke up this morning to the sound of weeping. Alwyn and Linden were in my room. They were crying because they could not find Mum and Dad. I was angry and told them that they weren't babies anymore. I said Mum and Dad would be back soon. I thought they must have run to town for something we needed.

But night has fallen and we are still alone. I've heard no word from our neighbors, none from Mum and Dad's coven. I went to Siobhan's house, and to Caradog Owens's house over in Grasmere, to ask if they knew where Mum and Dad were. But there was no one home.

And there's something else. When I was making my bed I found Dad's *lueg* under my pillow—the stone he uses to scry with. How did it get there? He always keeps it safe with the rest of his magickal tools. He never even let me touch it before.

So how did it get under my pillow? I have a bad feeling....

Dad has often told me that when he and Mum are on their errands, I am master of the house. It is my job to watch over my brother and sister. But I am not a man like him. I am only eight years old. I won't be a witch for many years yet. What can I do if there is trouble?

What if something happened to them? They have never left us alone like this. Did someone take them away? Are they being held prisoner somewhere?

I must sleep, but I can't. Alwyn and Linden can sleep for me. I must be strong for them.

Mum and Dad will come back to us soon. They will. I know it.

Goddess, bring them home.

—Giomanach

As if he sensed our approach, Hunter stood quickly. His green eyes were puffy and bloodshot. His face was pale from the cold, and snowflakes had settled on his hat. But aside from the redness of his eyes, he looked like he was carved of marble—still and somehow dangerous. Why was he looking under the car? More important, why did I find him so threatening? I didn't know the answers, but I knew that as a blood witch, I should trust my instincts. I shuddered inside my coat.

"What are you doing, Niall?" Cal demanded. His voice was so low and steady that I hardly recognized it. I looked at him and saw that his jaw was tight. His hands were clenched at his sides.

"Just admiring your big American car," Hunter said. He sniffed, then pulled a handkerchief from his pocket. He must have a cold, I thought. I wondered how long he'd been out here in the snow.

Cal flicked his gaze to the Explorer, sweeping it from bumper to bumper, as if scanning for something out of place.

"Hello, Morgan," Hunter murmured. With his sickly nasal voice the greeting sounded like an insult. "Interesting company you keep."

The falling snowflakes were cold against my hot skin.

I shifted my books to my other arm and gazed at Hunter, confused. Why should he care?

Hunter stepped onto the sidewalk. Cal turned to face him, placing himself between me and Hunter. My hero, I thought. But a part of me still felt a palpable fear as well. Hunter scowled, his cheekbones so sharp that snowflakes seemed to glance off them.

"So Cal is teaching you the secrets of Wicca, is he?" he asked. He leaned nonchalantly against the hood of the car, and Cal didn't take his eyes off him for a second. "Of course, he has quite a few secrets of his own, eh?"

"You can leave now, Niall," Cal spat.

"No, I think not," Hunter replied evenly. "I think I'll be around for a while. Who knows, I might have to teach Morgan a thing or two myself."

"What is that supposed to mean?" I asked.

Hunter just shrugged.

"Get away from me," Cal commanded.

Hunter stood back with a slight smile, his hands in the air as if to show he was unarmed. Cal glanced from him to the car. I'd never seen Cal so angry, so on the verge of losing control. It frightened me. He was like a tiger, waiting to pounce.

"There is one thing you should learn, Morgan," Hunter remarked. "Cal isn't the only blood witch around. He'd like to think he's a big man, but he's really just small fry. One day you'll realize that. And I want to be there to see it."

"Go to hell," Cal spat.

"Look, you don't *know* me," I told Hunter loudly. "You don't know anything about me. So shut up and leave us alone!" I stomped angrily to the car. But as I pushed past Hunter, barely brushing against him, a sickening rush of energy hit me in my stomach—so hard that I gasped. He's put a spell on me, I thought in a panic, groping for the door handle. But he'd said nothing; he'd done nothing that I could see. I blinked hard.

"Please, Cal," I whispered, my voice shaking. "Let's go."

Cal was still staring at Hunter as if he'd like to rip him apart. His eyes blazed, and his skin seemed to whiten.

Hunter stared back, but I felt his concentration break: he was shaken for a moment. Then he steeled himself again.

"Please, Cal," I repeated. I knew something had happened to me; I felt hot and strange and desperate to be gone, to be at home. My voice must have alerted Cal to my distress because he took his eyes off Hunter for a second. I stared at him pleadingly. Finally he pulled his keys from his pocket, slid into the car, and opened my door.

I collapsed inside and put my hands over my face.

"Good-bye, Morgan!" Hunter called.

Cal gunned the engine and sped backward, shooting snow and ice toward Hunter. I peeked through my fingers and saw Hunter standing there with an indecipherable expression on his face. Was it . . . anger? No. Snow swirled around him as he watched us leave.

It wasn't until we were almost at my house that it suddenly hit me.

The look on his face had been hunger.

5.
Dagda

Beltane, 1992

I feel like punching everyone and everything. I hate my life, hate living with Uncle Beck and Aunt Shelagh. Nothing has been the same, not since Mum and Dad disappeared that day two years ago, and it never will be.

Today Linden fell off Uncle Beck's ladder and bloodied his knee. I had to clean him up and bandage the wound, and all the while he wept. And I cursed Mum and Dad while I did it, I cursed them for leaving us and leaving me to do their job. Why did they go? Where did they go? Uncle Beck knows, but he won't tell me. He says I am not ready. Aunt Shelagh says he's only thinking of my good. But how can it be good not to know the truth? I hate Uncle Beck.

In the end, when I was finished with Linden, I made a face, and he laughed through his tears. That made me feel better.

But only for a while. No happiness lasts very long. That's what I've learned. Linden would do well to learn it, too.

—Giomanach

Mom came into my room that night as I was getting dressed to go to Jenna Ruiz's for the circle. "Are you guys going to a movie?" she asked. She automatically began straightening the pile of rejected clothes on my bed.

"No," I said, and left it at that. When it came to Wicca, silence was the best policy. I turned in front of the mirror, frowning. As usual, I looked hopeless. I pulled open the bathroom door and yelled, "Mary K.!" Having an endlessly trendy sister had its perks.

She appeared at once.

I held out my arms. "Help."

Her warm brown eyes skimmed me critically, then she shook her head. "Take it all off," she ordered.

I obeyed meekly. Mom grinned at us.

While Mary K. pawed through my closet, Mom tried to wheedle more information from me. "You said you were going to Jenna's? Will Bree be there?"

I paused for a moment. Both Mary K. and Mom had mentioned Bree today. I wasn't really surprised; she had been a virtual fixture at our house for years—but talking about her was painful. "I don't think so," I finally said. "It's just going to be our regular group, getting together. You know, I've never been to Jenna's house before." A lame attempt to change the subject, I knew. Mary K. threw a pair of skinny jeans at me, and I obediently shimmied into them.

"We never see Bree anymore," Mom commented as Mary K. disappeared into her room.

I nodded, aware of Mom's eyes on me.

"Did you guys have a fight?" Mom asked straight out.

Mary K. returned, holding an embroidered cotton sweater.

"Kind of," I said with a sigh. I really didn't want to get into this, not now. I pulled off my sweatshirt and tugged on the sweater. It fit smoothly, to my surprise. I'm taller and thinner than Mary K., but she inherited my mom's curvy chest. My adoptive mom, that is. I wondered fleetingly if Maeve Riordan had been built like me.

"Did you fight over Wicca?" Mom pried with the subtlety of an ax. "Does Bree not like Wicca?"

"No," I said, pulling my hair out of the sweater and examining my new look. It was a big improvement, which lifted my mood a little. "Bree does Wicca, too." I sighed again, finally giving in to Mom's interrogation. "Actually, we fought over Cal. She wanted to go out with him, but he wanted to go out with me. Now she pretty much hates me."

Mom was quiet for a moment. Mary K. stared at the floor.

"That's too bad," Mom said after a moment. "It's sad when friends fight over a boy." She laughed gently, reassuringly. "Usually the boys aren't worth it."

I nodded. A lump had formed in my throat. I didn't want to talk about Bree anymore; it hurt too much. I checked the clock. "I wish it didn't have to be like this. Anyway, I'm late; I better go." My voice was strained. "Thanks, Mary K." I kissed the air beside Mom's cheek—then I was down the stairs and out the door, pulling on my coat and shivering in the cold.

In a few moments, though, the sadness over Bree began to melt away. I felt a tingle of anticipation. It was circle night.

Jenna lived not far from me in a small, Victorian-style house. It was charmingly run-down, with an overgrown yard. The paint was peeling, and one shutter was missing a hinge.

As soon as I walked up the steps to the porch, a cat greeted me. It meowed and rubbed its head against my legs.

"What are you doing out here?" I whispered as I rang the doorbell.

Jenna opened the door right away, her cheeks flushed, blond hair pulled back, a big smile on her face.

"Hi, Morgan!" she said, then looked down at the cat squeezing its way inside. "Hugo, I told you it was freezing out there! I called you! You ignored me. Now your paws are cold."

I laughed and glanced around to see who was here. No Cal, not yet. Of course, I knew that already; I hadn't seen his car outside, hadn't felt his presence. Robbie was examining Jenna's stereo system, which had a real turntable. A stack of old vinyl records was piled haphazardly next to the fireplace.

"Hey," he said.

"Hi," I answered. I was amazed that this was Jenna's home. Jenna was by far one of the most popular girls in school and thoroughly up-to-date, like Mary K.—but her house looked like a throwback to the 1970s. The furniture was comfortably shabby, with plants hung in front of every window, some needing water. There seemed to be dust and cat hair everywhere. And dog hair, I amended, seeing two basset hounds snoring on a dog bed in a corner of the dining room. No wonder Jenna has asthma, I found myself thinking. She'd have to live in a plastic bubble in this house to breathe clean air.

"Want some cider?" Jenna asked, handing me a cup. It was warm and smelled deliciously spicy. I took a sip as the doorbell rang again.

"Hey!" It was Sharon Goodfine. She shrugged off her thick black leather coat and hung it on the stairs' newel post. "Hugo! Don't even think about it!" she cried as the cat reached up to pat her coat with his fat white paws. Obviously she had been here before.

Ethan Sharp came right after Sharon, looking underdressed in a thin fatigue jacket.

Sharon handed him a cup of cider. "Apparently you lack the gene that allows you to dress for the weather," she teased.

He grinned at her, looking vaguely stoned, even though I knew he didn't smoke pot anymore. She smiled back. I tried not to roll my eyes. When would they realize that they liked each other? Right now they sort of sniped at each other childishly.

Cal arrived next, and my heart lifted as he walked through the door. I was still upset about what had happened with Hunter at Practical Magick; Cal and I had hardly said two words to each other on the way home. But seeing him now made me feel much better, and when he met my eyes, I could tell he had missed me in the hours we had been apart.

"Morgan, can I talk to you for a second?" he asked, hesitating near the door. He didn't have to add "alone." I could see it in his face.

I nodded, surprised, and stepped toward him.

"What's up?" I asked.

Turning his back on the living room, he pulled a small stone from his pocket. It was smooth, round, and gray—about the size of a Ping-Pong ball. Inscribed on it in black ink was a rune. I had been reading about runes, so I recognized it instantly: it was Peorth, the rune for hidden things revealed.

"I found this stuck into the suspension of my car," Cal whispered.

My head jerked up in alarm. "Did Hunter . . . ?" I didn't finish.

Cal nodded.

"What does it mean?" I asked.

"It means that he's using dirty tricks to spy on us," he muttered, shoving the stone back into his pocket. "It's nothing to worry about, though. If anything, it proves that he doesn't have much power."

"But—"

"Don't worry," Cal said. He flashed me a reassuring smile. "You know, I don't even know why I bothered showing this to you. It's not a big deal. Really."

I watched him as he headed to the living room to say hi to the others. He wasn't being completely honest with me; I could feel that even without using my heightened witch senses. Hunter's little trick did concern him, at least to some degree.

What is Hunter up to? I wondered again. What does he want with us?

It was already nine o'clock, when we usually got started. We drank cider. Robbie played music. I tried to forget about the stone. Looking at the pets soothed me: the dogs snored and twitched in their sleep, and the cats rubbed our legs in quiet demands for attention. I realized that the only one of us missing was Jenna's boyfriend, Matt. Jenna kept glancing at the tall grandfather clock in the foyer. As the minutes went by, she seemed increasingly ill at ease.

Her parents wandered in, met us, totally unconcerned with the fact that we were here to perform a Wiccan circle. It must be nice not to worry about making your parents mad, I thought. They headed upstairs to watch TV and told us to have a good time.

"Well, I'll get started with the circles," Cal said finally, opening his bag and settling down on the floor. "We'll give Matt ten more minutes."

"It's not like him to be late," Jenna murmured. "I called his cell phone, but it went straight to voice mail."

I suddenly remembered seeing Matt's car, parked next to Raven's. Was that only this morning? It had been a long day. I stifled a yawn as I sat on the worn green couch in the living room, watching Cal work.

"What are you doing?" I asked. Usually he drew a simple, perfect circle in salt. When we stepped in, he closed it and purified it with earth, air, fire, and water. But tonight's circle was different.

"This is more complicated," Cal explained.

Slowly the others drifted over to watch him. He was drawing circles within circles, leaving an opening in each one. There were three geometrically perfect circles now, the largest one taking up every inch of available space in Jenna's living room.

At the four compass points of the circles Cal drew a rune in chalk and also in the air: Mann, the rune for community and interdependence; Daeg, symbolizing dawn, awakening, clarity; Ur, for strength; Tyr, for victory in battle. Cal named them as he drew them but didn't offer any explanation. Before we could ask, the front door blew open and Matt breezed in, looking uncharacteristically disheveled and scattered.

"Hi, everyone. Sorry I'm late. Car trouble." He kept his head down, not meeting anyone's eye. Jenna looked at him, first in concern, then in confusion as he threw off his coat and came to watch Cal. For a moment Jenna hesitated. Then she walked up to him and took his hand. He gave her a brief smile but ignored her otherwise.

"Okay, everyone, step inside, and I'll close the circles," Cal instructed.

We did. I stood between Matt and Sharon. I tried never to stand next to Cal at a circle—I knew from experience that it would be too much to handle or control. Sharon and Matt were safe.

"Tonight we're working on personal goals," Cal continued, standing up. He handed Ethan a small bowl of salt and told him to purify the circle. Next he asked Jenna to light the incense, symbolizing air, and Sharon to touch each of our foreheads with a drop of water from its matching bowl. There was a fire in the living-room fireplace—and we used it for fire, naturally. My tiredness started to fade as I glanced around at everyone united for the same purpose. This circle felt special somehow, more important, more focused.

"During our breathing exercises," Cal said, "I want you each to concentrate on your own personal goals. Think about what you want out of Wicca and what you can offer to Wicca. Try to make it as simple and pure as possible. Stuff like 'I want a new car' isn't it."

We laughed.

"It's more like, I want to be more patient, or I want to be more honest, or I want to be braver. Think about what that means to you and how Wicca can help you achieve it. Any questions?"

I shook my head. There were so many things about myself I wanted to improve. I pictured myself as a smiling, confident person—open and honest and giving: a poster girl for Wicca. Feeling no anger, no envy, no greed. I sighed. Yeah, right. Accomplishing all that was a pretty ambitious project. Maybe too ambitious.

"Everyone take hands, and let's begin our breathing exercises," said Cal.

I reached for my neighbors. Matt's hand was still cool from being outside. Sharon's bracelets jingled against my wrist. I began to breathe slowly and deeply, trying to let all the day's negativity and tensions drain from my body, trying to draw in all the positive energies I could. I consciously relaxed every muscle, starting at the top of my head and working my way down. Within a few minutes I felt calm and focused, in a meditative state where I was only semiaware of my surroundings. This was good.

"Now think about your goals." Cal's voice seemed to float from everywhere at once. Unbidden, we began to move in a circle, first slowly, then more quickly and smoothly. My eyes opened, and I saw Jenna's living room as a series of dark smudges, a wild blur as we spun around and around. The fireplace marked our turns, and I looked into the fire, feeling its warmth and light and power.

"I want to be more open," I heard Sharon murmur, as if on a breeze.

"I want to be happy," said Ethan.

There was a moment of silence while I thought about what I wanted, and then Jenna said, "I want to be more lovable."

I felt Matt's hand clench mine for an instant, and then he said, "I want to be more honest." The words sounded reluctant and pained.

"I want to be strong," Cal whispered.

"I want to be a good person," said Robbie—and I thought, But you are.

I was last. I could feel the seconds ticking by. I still didn't know what I needed to work on the most. Yet words seemed to explode from my mouth, as if by their own accord. They hung on the air like smoke from a bog fire.

"I want to realize my power."

As soon as I said it, a current ran through the circle, like a wind whipping a rope. It was electric: it charged me, so that I felt I could fly or dance above the earth.

A chant came to my lips, one I didn't remember ever hearing or reading. I had no idea what it meant, but I let it flow from me, as my wish had flowed from me.

> *An di allaigh an di aigh*
> *An di allaigh an di ne ullah*
> *An di ullah be nith rah*
> *Cair di na ulla nith rah*
> *Cair feal ti theo nith rah*
> *An di allaigh an di aigh.*

I chanted it by myself, very softly at first—then more loudly, hearing my voice weaving a beautiful pattern in the air. The words sounded Gaelic and ancient. Someone was speaking through me. I lost myself, but I wasn't frightened. I was exhilarated. I threw my arms up in the air and swirled in circles within our circle. Together the coven spun in orbit; they were planets around a shining star—and the shining star was me. Silver rain was sprinkling down on my head, making me a goddess. My hair came undone from its tidy braid and whirled in a stream, catching the firelight. I was all-powerful, all-knowing, all-seeing—a goddess indeed. It came to me that the words must have been a spell, an ancient spell, one that called power.

It had called power to me tonight.

"Let's take it down."

The voice belonged to Cal. Again his words seemed to come from everywhere and nowhere at once. In answer to his bidding I slowed my whirling and let myself come to a wavering stop. I was as old as time itself; I was every woman who had ever danced for magick under the moon, every goddess who had celebrated life and death and the joy and sorrow in between.

Hunter Niall's face suddenly flashed into my mind, his superior, contemptuous smirk. Look at me, Hunter! I wanted to shout. Look at my power! I am a match for you or any witch!

Then, all at once, with no warning, I felt frightened, no longer in control. Without Cal telling me, I immediately lay face down on Jenna's wooden floor—with my hands flat by my shoulders to ground my energy. The wood was warm and smooth beneath my cheek, and energy flowed over and around me like water.

Slowly, very slowly, my breathing returned to normal. The fear fluttered, weakening. I became aware that someone was taking my right hand.

I blinked and glanced up. It was Jenna.

"Please," she said, placing my hand on her breastbone. I knew that she wanted me to help her. A week ago I had sent energy into her and eased her asthma. But I didn't think I had the power left now to do anything. Still, I closed my eyes and concentrated on light . . . white, healing light. I gathered it within me and sent it coursing down my arm, through my hand, into Jenna's constricted lungs. She breathed deeply, exclaiming slightly at the warmth.

"Thank you," she murmured.

I was lying on my side now. Suddenly I noticed that everyone was staring at me. Once again I was the center of attention. Self-consciously I pulled my hand away, wondering why a minute ago it was so natural to dance alone in front of everyone while now I felt embarrassed and shy. Why couldn't I hold on to those wonderful feelings of strength?

Matt put his hands on Jenna's shoulders, the most attention he'd shown her since he'd arrived. He was panting slightly from the effort of the dance.

"Did Morgan help your breathing?" he asked.

Jenna nodded, a blissful smile on her lips.

Cal crouched by my side, his hand on my hip.

"Everything all right?" he asked. He sounded excited, breathless.

"Uh . . . yeah," I murmured.

"Where did the chant come from?" he asked, brushing my hair off my shoulder. "What did it do?"

"I don't know where it came from, but it seemed to call power to me," I said.

"It was so beautiful," said Jenna.

"Pretty witchy," said Sharon.

"It was really cool," said Ethan.

I looked at Robbie, and he gazed calmly back at me, warm satisfaction on his face. I smiled at him. At that moment I was perfectly content—but the mood was abruptly broken when I felt nails on the back of my legs.

"Ow!" I muttered.

Half sitting up, I looked over to see the fuzzy, triangular head of a tiny gray kitten.

It mewed in greeting, and I laughed.

Jenna grinned. "Oh, sorry. One of our cats had kittens two months ago. We're trying to get rid of them. Anyone want a cat?" she joked.

I picked him up. He looked back at me intently, a world of feline wisdom in his baby blue eyes. He was solid gray, shorthaired, with a fat baby's belly and a short spiky tail that stuck straight up like an exclamation mark. He mewed in my face again and reached out a paw to pat my cheek.

"Hello," I said, remembering Maeve's kitten from her Book of Shadows. His name had been Dagda. I gazed at Jenna's cat in wonder, suddenly knowing that he was meant for me, that this was a perfect way to end the evening.

"Hi," I said softly. "Your name is Dagda, and you're going to come home and live with me. All right?"

He mewed once more, and I fell in love.

6.
Communion

Imbolc, 1993

A Seeker is here. He came two days ago and took a room above the pub on Goose Lane. He talked with Uncle Beck a good while yesterday. Uncle Beck says he'll talk with everyone and that we all have to be honest. But I don't like the man. His skin is white and he doesn't smile, and when he looks at me, his eyes are like two black holes. He makes me feel cold as frost.

—Giomanach

"A rat!" Mary K. screeched the next morning, right in my face. Not the best way to wake up. "Oh God, Morgan, there's a rat! Don't move!"

Of course by now I was stirring in my bed, and little Dagda was, too. He huddled next to me, small ears flat, body hunkered down. But he summoned enough courage to give Mary K. a good hiss. I wrapped my hand around him protectively.

Mom and Dad ran into my room, wide-eyed.

"It isn't a rat," I croaked, clearing sleep out of my throat.

"It isn't?" Dad asked.

I sat up. "It's a kitten," I said, stating the obvious. "Jenna's cat had kittens, and they were trying to get rid of them, so I took one. Can I keep him? I'll pay for his food and litter and everything," I added.

Dagda rose up on his little legs and eyed my family curiously. Then, as if to prove how cute he really was, he opened his mouth and mewed. They all melted at once. I hid a smile.

Mary K. sat on my bed and gently extended her hand. Dagda cautiously made his way across my comforter and licked her finger. Mary K. giggled.

"He's very sweet," said my mom. "How old is he?"

"Eight weeks," I said. "Old enough to leave his mom. So—is it okay?"

Mom and Dad exchanged a glance.

"Morgan, cats cost more than just food and litter," my dad said. "They need shots, checkups. . . ."

"He'll need to be neutered," my mom added.

I grinned. "Fortunately, we have a vet in the family," I said, referring to my aunt Eileen's girlfriend. "Besides, I have money saved from working last summer. I can pay for all that."

Mom and Dad both shrugged, then smiled.

"I guess it's okay, then," said Mom. "Maybe after church we can go to the store and get the stuff he needs."

"He's hungry," Mary K. announced, holding him to her chest. She immediately hopped up and dashed from the room, cradling him like a baby. "There's chicken left over from last night. I'll get him some."

"Don't give him milk," I called after her. "It'll upset his tummy. . . ."

I leaned back against my pillow, happy. Dagda was an official member of our family.

It was the second-to-last Sunday before Thanksgiving, so our church was decorated with dried leaves, pyracantha branches with bright red berries, pinecones, and rust-colored mums in pots. The atmosphere was beautiful, warm, and inviting. I decided it would be nice to find natural decorations like that for our own house at Thanksgiving.

In some way, I guess because I still wasn't sure about how coming to church fit in with Wicca, I felt strangely detached from everything going on around me. I stood when I was supposed to and knelt at the right time; I even followed along in the prayers and sang the hymns. But I did it without being a part of the congregation. My thoughts roamed freely, without restraint.

A thin, wintry sunlight had broken through the clouds. Yesterday's snow had mostly melted, and the church's stained-glass windows glowed with fiery reds, deep blues, pure greens, and crystalline yellows. There was a faint aroma of incense, and as I sank deeper within myself, I felt the weight of the people all around me. Their thoughts began to intrude, their hearts beating incessantly. I took a deep breath and shut my eyes, closing myself off to them.

Only when I had walled them out of my senses did I open my eyes again. I felt peaceful and full of gladness. The music was lovely, the ecclesiastical words moving. It all seemed timeless and traditional. It wasn't the bark and earth and salt of Wicca, nor was it the grounding of energy and the working of spells. But it was beautiful, in its own way.

I rose automatically when it was time to take communion. I followed my parents and sister up to the railing in front of the altar. The tall altar candles burned brightly, reflecting off the brass fixtures and dark polished wood. I knelt on the flat needle-work pillow that had been embroidered by the women's guild. My mom had made one of these pillows a couple of years ago.

My hands clasped, I waited as Father Hotchkiss said the wine blessing for every person in the row. I felt at peace. Already I was looking forward to going home to see Dagda, read Maeve's Book of Shadows, and do some more rune research. Last night when Cal had drawn runes in the air around our circle, it seemed to focus our energy in a whole new way. I liked runes and wanted to find out more about them.

Next to me Mary K. took a sip of wine. I caught a whiff of the fruity scent. A moment later it was my turn. Father Hotchkiss stood in front of me, wiping the large silver chalice with a linen cloth.

"This is the blood of Christ our Lord," he murmured. "Drink this in his name, that you may be saved."

I tilted my head forward to sip.

With an unexpected stumble Father Hotchkiss lurched toward me. The chalice slipped from his hands. It dropped to the white marble floor with a metallic clang, and Father Hotchkiss gripped the wooden rail that separated us.

I put my hand on his, searching his face. "Are you okay, Father?" I asked.

He nodded. "I'm sorry, my dear. I slipped. Did I splash you?"

"No, no." I looked down, and sure enough, my dress was wine free. Deacon Carlson was hurrying to get another blessed chalice, and Father Hotchkiss stepped away to help him.

Mary K. was waiting for me, looking uncertain. I stayed kneeling, watching the dark red wine flow across the white marble floor. The contrast of color was mesmerizing.

"What happened?" Mary K. whispered. "Are you okay?"

That was when the thought came to me: What if I was the one who had made Father Hotchkiss stumble? I almost gasped, with my hand over my mouth. What if, in the middle of all my Wicca thoughts, a force had decreed that my taking communion was not a good idea? Quickly I stood, my eyes large. Mary K. headed back to our pew and our parents, and I followed her.

No, I thought. It was just a coincidence. It didn't mean anything.

But inside me a witchy voice said sweetly: There are no coincidences. And everything means something.

So *what* did it mean, exactly? That I should stop taking communion? That I should stop coming to church altogether? I glanced at my mother, who smiled at me with no awareness of the confusion that was raging inside me. I was thankful for that.

I couldn't imagine cutting church out of my life completely. Catholicism was part of the glue that held our family together; it was a part of *me*. But maybe I should hold off on taking communion for a while, at least until I figured out what it all meant. I could still come to church. I could still participate. Couldn't I?

I sighed as I sat back down beside Mary K. She looked at me but didn't say anything.

With every door that Wicca opened, I thought, another door seemed to shut. Somehow I had to find balance.

After lunch at the Widow's Diner we stopped at the grocery store. I bought a litter box and a scoop, a box of cat litter, and a bag of kitten food. Mom and Dad pitched in for a couple of cat toys, and Mary K. bought some kitty treats.

I was really touched, and I hugged them all, right in the pet aisle.

Of course, when we got home, we found that Dagda had peed on my down comforter. He had also eaten part of Mom's maidenhair fern and barfed it up on the carpet. Then he had apparently worked himself into a frenzy sharpening his tiny but amazingly effective claws on the armrest of my dad's favorite chair.

Now he was asleep on a pillow, curled up like a fuzzy little snail.

"God, he's so *cute*," I said, shaking my head.

7.
Symbols

I had to draw a spell of protection tonight. I invoked the Goddess and drew the runes at the four points of the compass: Ur, Sigel, Eolh, and Tyr. I took iron nails and buried them at the four corners, wearing a gold ring. And from now on, I will carry a piece of malachite for protection.

A Seeker is here.

But I am not afraid. The first blow has already been struck, and the Seeker is weakened by it. And as the Seeker weakens, my love grows stronger and stronger.

   —Sgàth

On Monday, Mary K. and I were late for school. I had stayed up late reading Maeve's BOS, and Mary K. had stayed up late having a heartfelt, tortured talk with Bakker—and so we both overslept. We signed ourselves in at the office and got our tardy slips: the New York Public School System's version of the Scarlet Letter.

The halls were empty as we split up for our lockers and headed toward our respective homerooms. My mind swam with what I had been reading. Maeve had loved the herbal side of Wicca. Her BOS was filled with several long passages about magickal uses for plants—and how they're affected by time of year, amount of recent rainfall, position of stars, and phases of the moon. I wondered if I was a descendant of the Brightendale clan, the clan that farmed the earth for healing powers.

In homeroom I slithered into my desk chair. Out of habit I glanced at Bree, but she ignored me, and I felt irritated that it still caused me grief. Forget her, I thought. I'd once read somewhere that it takes about half as long to recover from a deep relationship as the relationship lasted. So in Bree's case, I would still be upset about her a good six years from now. Great.

I thought about Dagda and how Bree would adore him: she'd loved her cat Smokey and had been devastated when he died, two days after her fourteenth birthday. I'd helped her bury him in her backyard.

"Hey. Slept late?" my friend Tamara Pritchett called softly from the next desk. It seemed as if I barely saw her anymore, now that Wicca was taking up so much of my time.

I nodded and started organizing my books and notebooks for my morning classes.

"Well, you missed the big news," Tamara went on. I looked up. "Ben and Janice are officially going out. Boyfriend and girlfriend."

"Really? Oh, cool," I said. I glanced across the room at the lovebirds in question. They were sitting next to each other, talking quietly, smiling at each other. I felt happy for them. But I also felt removed—they, too, were friends I'd hardly seen in recent weeks.

My senses prickled, and I glanced across to see Bree's dark eyes on me. I was startled by their intense expression, and then we both blinked and it was gone. She turned away, and I was unsure if I had imagined it or not. I felt unsettled. Cal had said there was no dark side to Wicca. But aren't two sides of a circle opposite each other? And if one side was good, what was the other? I had disliked Sky as soon as I had met her. What was Bree doing with her?

The bell rang for first period. I felt sour, as if I shouldn't be there—and thought enviously of Dagda at home, wreaking feline havoc.

During American lit it started to drizzle outside: a depressing, steady stream that was trying hard to turn into sleet but not quite making it. My eyelids felt heavy. I hadn't even had time for a Diet Coke yet. I pictured my bed at home and for just a moment considered getting Cal, skipping out, and going home to be alone with him. We could lie in my bed, reading Maeve's BOS and talking about magick. . . .

Major temptation. By lunchtime I was really torn, even though I never skipped school. Only the knowledge that my mom sometimes popped home in the middle of the day prevented me from bringing up the idea to Cal when I saw him.

"You bought lunch?" he asked, eyeing my tray as I slid it onto our lunch table. He met my eyes. As clear as the rainfall, I heard the words *I missed you this morning* inside my head.

I smiled and nodded, sitting down across from him, next to Sharon. "I overslept, so I didn't have time to make anything at home."

"Hey, Morgan," Jenna said, brushing her wheat-colored hair over her shoulder. "You know what I've been thinking about? Those words you said the other night. They were so amazing. I still can't get them out of my mind."

I shrugged. "Yeah, it's funny. I don't know where they came from," I said, popping the top off my soda. "I haven't had time to research it, either. At the time I thought it felt like a spell, calling power to me. But I don't know. The words sounded really old."

Sharon smiled tentatively. "It was kind of creepy, to tell you the truth," she murmured. She opened her container of soup and took out a crusty roll. "I mean, it was beautiful, but it's weird to have words you don't even know coming out of your mouth."

I looked up at Cal. "Did you recognize them?"

He shook his head. "Uh-uh. But later I thought about it, and I felt like I had heard them before. I wish I had taped our circle. I could play it for Mom and see if she knew what it was."

"Cool, you're speaking in tongues," Ethan joked. "Like that girl in *The Exorcist.*"

I pursed my lips. "Great," I said, and Robbie laughed.

Cal shot me an amused glance. "Want some?" he asked, handing me a slice of his apple.

Without thinking, I took a bite. It was astonishingly

delicious. I looked at it: it was just an apple slice. But it was tart and sweet, bursting with juice.

"This is a *great* apple," I said, amazed. "It's perfect. It's the *über*-apple."

"Apples are very symbolic," said Cal. "Especially of the Goddess. Look." He took his pocketknife and cut his apple again—but across the middle instead of top to bottom. He held up a piece. "A pentacle," he said pointing to the pattern made from the seeds. It was a five-pointed star within the circle of the apple's skin.

"Whoa," I said.

"Awesome," said Matt. Jenna glanced at him, but he didn't meet her eye.

"Everything means something," said Cal lightly, taking a bite of the apple. I looked up at him sharply, reminded of what had happened yesterday in church.

Across the lunchroom I saw Bree sitting with Raven, Lin Green, Chip Newton, and Beth Nielson. I wondered if Bree was enjoying hanging out with her new crowd . . . people she had once referred to as stoners, wastoids. Her old crowd—Nell Norton, Alessandra Spotford, Justin Bartlett, and Suzanne Herbert—were sitting at a table near the windows. They probably thought Bree was crazy.

"I wonder how their coven's circle went on Saturday," I mumbled, half to myself. "Bree's and Raven's. Robbie, do you know? Did you talk to Bree?"

Robbie shrugged and finished his piece of pizza.

"It went really well," said Matt absently. Then he blinked and frowned a tiny bit, as if he hadn't expected to say anything.

Jenna looked at him. "How do you know?" she asked.

Matt's face turned slightly pink. He shrugged, his attention on his lunch. "Uh, I talked to Raven during English," he said finally. "She said it was cool."

Jenna regarded Matt steadily. She started to gather up her tray. Once again I remembered seeing Matt's car and Raven's car on the side of the road. As I wondered what it could mean, I heard Mary K.'s laughter, a few tables away. She was sitting next to Bakker with her friend Jaycee, Jaycee's older sister, Brenda, and a bunch of their friends. Mary K. and Bakker were looking into each other's eyes. I shook my head. He had won her over. But he'd better watch his step.

"What are you doing this afternoon?" Cal asked in the parking lot after school. The rain had all but stopped, and an icy wind was blowing.

I glanced at my watch. "Besides waiting for my sister? Nothing. I have to get dinner together."

Robbie snaked his way through a few cars, heading toward us. "Hey, what's going on with Matt?" he called. "He's acting all squirrelly."

"Yeah, I thought so, too, " I said. "Almost like he wants to break up with Jenna but doesn't want to at the same time. If that makes any sense."

Cal smiled. "I don't know them as well as you guys do," he said, putting his arm around me. "Is Matt acting that different?"

Robbie nodded. "Yeah. Not that we're bosom buddies or anything, but he seems kind of off to me. Usually he's really straightforward. He's always just right there." He gestured with his hands.

"I know," I agreed. "Now he seems to have something else going on." I wanted to mention the Matt-Raven car thing but thought it would be too gossipy. I wasn't even sure if it meant anything. I suddenly wished Bree and I were still close. She would have appreciated the significance.

"Morgan!" called Jaycee. "Mary K. asked me to tell you that she was catching a ride with Bakker." Jaycee waved and trotted off, her blond ponytail bouncing.

"Damn!" I said, disengaging myself from Cal. "I have to get home."

"What's the matter? Do you want me to come with you?" Cal asked.

"I would love it," I said gratefully. It would be nice to have an ally in case Bakker needed to be kicked out of the house again.

"See you, Robbie," I called, hurrying off to my car. Damnation, Mary K., I thought. How stupid can you be?

8.
Muìrn Beatha Dàn

Ostara, 1993

Aunt Shelagh told me she saw someone under a braigh before, when she was a girl, visiting her granny in Scotland. A local witch had been selling potions and charms and spells to cause harm. When Aunt Shelagh was there one summer, the Seeker came.

Shelagh says she woke in the night to screams and howls. The whole village turned out to see the Seeker take away the herbwife. In the moonlight, Shelagh saw the glint of the silver braigh around the herbwife's wrists, saw how the flesh was burned. The Seeker took her away, and no one saw her again, though they whispered she was living on the streets in Edinburgh.

Shelagh doesn't think the woman was ever able to do magick again, good or bad, so I don't know how long she would have wanted to live like that. But Shelagh also said that one sight of that herbwife under the braigh was enough to make her promise to never ever misuse her power. It was a terrible thing, she said. Terrible to see. She told me this story last month, when the Seeker was here. But he took no one away with him, and our coven is placid once more.

I am glad he's gone.

—Giomanach

I drove home as quickly as I could, considering that the streets were basically one big ice slick. The temperature kept dropping, and the air was miserable with the kind of bone-drenching chill that Widow's Vale seems to specialize in.

"I thought Mary K. broke up with Bakker after what happened," said Cal.

"She did," I grumbled. "But he's been begging her to take him back, it was all a mistake, he's so sorry, it'll never happen again, blah blah blah." Anger made my voice shrill.

My tires skidded a bit as I turned into our driveway. Bakker's car was parked out front. I slammed the car door and crunched up our walk—only to find Mary K. and Bakker huddled together on the front steps, shaking and practically blue with cold.

"What are you doing?" I exclaimed, relief washing over me.

"I wanted to wait for you," Mary K. muttered, and I silently applauded her good sense.

"Come on, then," I said, pushing open the front door. "But you guys stay downstairs."

"Okay," Bakker mumbled, sounding half frozen. "As long as it's warm."

Cal started making hot cider for us all while I stayed outside and salted the front walk and the driveway so my parents wouldn't have a hard time when they got home. It was nice to get back inside, and I cranked up the thermostat, then headed to the kitchen. It was my night to make dinner. I washed four potatoes, stabbed them with a fork, and put them in the oven to bake.

"Hey, Morgan, can we just run upstairs for a sec?" Mary K. asked tentatively, clutching her mug. Since I'd met Cal, I'd begun drinking a ton of cider. It was incredibly warming on cold days. "All my CDs are in my room."

I shook my head. "Tough," I said shortly. I blew on my cider to cool it. "You guys stay downstairs, or Mom will have my ass."

Mary K. sighed. Then she and Bakker brought their stuff to the dining-room table and self-righteously started to do their homework. Or at least they pretended to do their homework.

As soon as my sister was gone, I waved my left hand in a circle, deosil, over my cider, and whispered, "Cool the fire." The next time I took a sip, it was just right, and I beamed. I loved being a witch!

Cal grinned and said, "Now what? Do we have to stay downstairs, too?"

I let my mind wander tantalizingly over the possibilities if I didn't practice what I preached but finally sighed and said, "I guess so. Mom would go insane if I was upstairs with an evil boy while she wasn't home. I mean, you've probably got only one thing on your mind and all."

"Yeah." Cal raised his eyebrows and laughed. "But it's one good thing, let me tell you."

Dagda padded into the kitchen and mewed.

"Hey, little guy," I crooned. I put my cider down on the counter and scooped him up. He began to purr hard, his small body trembling.

"He gets to go upstairs," Cal pointed out, "and he's a boy."

I grinned. "They don't care if *he* sleeps with me," I said.

Cal let out a good-natured groan as I carried Dagda into the family room and sat on the couch. Cal sat next to me, and I felt the warmth of his leg against mine. I smiled at him, but his face turned solemn. He stroked my hair and traced the line of my chin with his fingers.

"What's wrong?" I asked.

"You surprise me all the time," he said out of the blue.

"How?" I was stroking Dagda's soft triangular head, and he was purring and kneading my knees.

"You're just—different than I thought you would be," he said. He put his arm across the back of the couch and leaned toward me as if trying to memorize my face, my eyes. He seemed so serious.

I didn't know what to think. "What did you expect me to be like?" I asked. I could smell the clean laundry scent of his shirt. In my mind I pictured us stretched on the couch, kissing. We could do it. I knew that Mary K. and Bakker were in the other room, that they wouldn't bother us. But suddenly I felt insecure, remembering again that I was almost seventeen and he was the first boy who'd ever asked me out, ever kissed me. "Boring?" I asked. "Kind of vanilla?"

His golden eyes crinkled at the edges, and he tapped my

lips gently with one finger. "No, of course not," he said. "But you're so strong. So interesting." His forehead creased momentarily, as if he regretted what he'd said. "I mean, right when I met you, I thought you were interesting and good-looking and the rest of it, and I could tell right away you had a gift for the craft. I wanted to get close to you. But you've turned out to be so much more than that. The more I know you, the more you feel equal to me, like a real partner. Like I said, my muìrn beatha dàn. It's kind of a huge idea." He shook his head. "I've never felt this way before."

I didn't know what to say. I looked at his face, still amazed by how beautiful I found it, still awed by the feelings he awoke in me. "Kiss me," I heard myself breathe. He leaned closer and pressed his lips to mine.

After several moments Dagda shifted impatiently in my lap. Cal laughed and shook his head, then drew away from me as if deciding to exercise better judgment. He reached down and pulled a pad of paper and pen out of his book bag and handed them to me.

"Let's see you write your runes," he said.

I nodded. It wasn't kissing, but it was magick—a close second. I began to draw, from memory, the twenty-four runes. There were others, I knew, that dated from later times, but these twenty-four were considered the basics.

"Feoh," I said softly, drawing a vertical line, then two lines that slanted up and to the right from it. "For wealth."

"What else is it for?" asked Cal.

"Prosperity, increase, success." I thought. "Things turning out well. And this is Eolh, for protection," I said, drawing the shape that was like an upside-down Mercedes logo.

"It's very positive. This is Geofu, which stands for gift or partnership. Generosity. Strengthening friendships or other relationships. The joining of the God and Goddess."

"Very good," said Cal, nodding.

I kept on until I had drawn all of them, as well as a blank space for the Wyrd rune, the undrawn one, the symbol that signified something you ought not know: dangerous or hurtful knowledge, a path you should not take. In rune sets it was represented by a blank tile.

"That's great, Morgan," Cal whispered. "Now close your eyes and think about these runes. Let your fingers drift over the page, and stop when you feel you should stop. Then look at what rune you've stopped on."

I loved this kind of thing. I closed my eyes and let my fingers skim the paper. At first I felt nothing, but then I focused my concentration, trying to shut out everything except what I was doing. I tuned out the murmur of Mary K. and Bakker's voices from the dining room, the ticking of the cuckoo clock my dad had built from a kit, the gentle hum of the furnace kicking in.

I don't know how long it was before I realized that my fingertips were picking up impressions. I felt feathery softness, a cool stone, a warm prickle . . . were these the images of the runes? I let myself go deeper into the magick, losing myself in its power. *There*. Yes, there was one place where I felt a stronger sensation. Each time my fingers passed it, it called to me. I let my hand drift downward to rest on the paper and opened my eyes.

My fingers were on the rune called Yr. The symbol for death.

I frowned. "What does this mean?"

"Hmmm," said Cal, looking at the paper, his hand on his chin. "Well, you know, Yr can be interpreted many different ways. It doesn't mean that you or someone you know is going to die. It may simply mean the ending of something and the beginning of something new. Some sort of big change, not necessarily a bad one."

The double-fishhook symbol of Yr shone darkly on the white paper. Death. The importance of endings. It seemed like an omen. A scary omen. A jet of adrenaline surged through me, making my heart thud.

All at once I heard the back door open.

"Hello?" came my mom's voice. "Morgan? Mary K.?" There were footsteps in the dining room. My concentration evaporated.

"Hey, sweetie," she said to Mary K. She paused. "Hello, Bakker. Mary K., is your sister here?" I knew she meant: For God's sake, you're not here alone with a boy, are you?

"I'm in here," I said, tucking the paper of runes into my pocket. Cal and I walked out of the family room. Mom's eyes flashed over us, and I could immediately see the thoughts going through her mind. *My girls, alone in the house with two boys.* But we were all downstairs, we had our clothes on, and Mary K. and Bakker were at least sitting at the dining-room table. I could see Mom consciously decide not to worry about it.

"Are you baking potatoes?" she asked, sniffing.

"Yep," I said.

"Do you think we could mash them instead?" she asked. "I've asked Eileen and Paula to dinner." She held up a folder. "I've got some hot prospects for them housewise."

"Cool," I said. "Yeah, we can mash them, and then

there'll be enough. I'm making hamburgers, too, but there's plenty."

"Great. Thanks, sweetie." Mom headed upstairs to change out of her work clothes.

"I'd better go," I heard Bakker say reluctantly. Good, I thought.

"Me too," said Cal. "Bakker, do you think you could give me a lift back to school? That's where my car is."

"No prob," said Bakker.

I walked Cal outside, and we hugged on the front porch. He kissed my neck and whispered, "I'll call you later. Don't get all bent about the Yr thing. It was just an exercise."

"Okay," I whispered back, although I still wasn't sure how I felt. "Thanks for coming over."

Aunt Eileen arrived first. "Hi!" she said, coming in and taking off her coat. "Paula called and said she was running a few minutes late—something about a Chihuahua having a difficult labor."

I smiled awkwardly in the front hall. I hadn't seen her since I had demanded to know why she hadn't told me I was adopted, at a family dinner two weeks ago. I felt a little embarrassed to see her again, but I was sure Mom had been talking to her, keeping her up-to-date with everything.

"Hi, Aunt Eileen," I said. "I . . . uh, I'm sorry about making a scene last time. You know."

As if to answer, she swept me up in a tight hug. "It's okay, sweetie," she whispered. "I understand. I don't blame you a bit."

We pulled back and smiled at each other for a moment. I

knew Aunt Eileen would make everything okay again. Then she glanced down and gasped, pointing urgently to my dad's La-Z-Boy, where a small gray butt and tail were sticking out from under the skirt.

I laughed and scooped Dagda out.

"This is Dagda," I said, rubbing him behind his ears. "He's my new cat."

"Oh, my goodness," said Eileen, stroking his head. "I'm sorry. I thought he was a rat."

"You should know better," I joked, putting him back on the chair. "You *date* a vet."

Aunt Eileen laughed, too. "I know, I know."

Soon afterward Paula arrived, her sandy hair windblown, her nose pink with cold.

"Hey," I greeted her. "Is the Chihuahua okay?"

"Fine, and the proud mom of two pups," she said, giving me a hug. "Oh! What a beautiful kitten!" she said, spotting Dagda on Dad's chair.

I beamed. *Finally!* Somebody who knew what a treasure Dagda was. I'd always liked Aunt Eileen's new girlfriend, but now it struck me that they were a perfect match. Maybe Paula was even Eileen's muìrn beatha dàn.

Thinking about it brought a smile to my face. Everybody deserved somebody. Not everyone was as lucky as I was, of course. I had Cal.

9.
Trust

The magick is working, as I knew it would. The Seeker no longer frightens me as much. I believe I am the stronger of us two, especially with the power of the others behind me.

Soon I will join with my love. I do understand the urgency, though I wish they would trust me to do it my way, at my pace. More and more, lately, I want to do this for my own sake. But the timing must be perfect. I dare not frighten her; there is too much at stake.

I have been reading the ancient texts, the ones about love and union. I have even copied down my favorite passage from <u>Song of the Goddess</u>: "To give pleasure to yourself and to others, that is my ritual. To love yourself and others, that is my ritual. Celebrate your body and spirit with joy and passion, and as you do so, you worship me."

—Sgàth

"I hope you know that you can't trust Bakker," I said to Mary K. the next morning. I tried not to sound snotty, but it came out that way anyhow.

Mary K. didn't answer. She just looked out her car window. Frost covered everything in lacy, powdered-sugar patterns.

I drove slowly, trying to avoid the hard patches of black ice where the newly plowed roads had puddled and frozen. My breath came out in a mist inside Das Boot.

"I know he's really sorry," I went on, in spite of my sister's stiff face. "And I believe he really cares about you. But I just don't trust his temper."

"Then don't go out with him," Mary K. muttered.

Alarm bells went off in my brain. I was criticizing him, and she was defending him. I was doing what I feared: pushing them closer together. I took a deep breath. Goddess, guide me, I said silently.

"You know," I said finally, several blocks from school. "I bet you're right. I bet it was just a onetime thing. But you guys have talked, right?" I didn't wait for an answer. "And he *is* really sorry. I guess it will never happen again."

Mary K. looked over at me suspiciously, but I kept my face neutral and my eyes on the road.

"He *is* sorry," my sister said. "He feels terrible about it. He never meant to hurt me. And now he knows he has to listen to me."

I nodded. "I know he cares about you."

"He does," said Mary K.

She looked transparently self-assured. Inside, my heart throbbed. I hated this. Maybe everything I had just said was true. But I couldn't help fearing that Bakker would try again to force Mary K. into doing something she didn't want to do.

If he did, I would make him pay.

I got to school early enough to see Cal before the bell rang. He was waiting for me by the east entrance, where our coven gathered during better weather.

"Hey," he said, kissing me. "Come on, we found a new place to hang out. It's warmer."

Inside, we passed the steps leading to the second floor and turned a corner. There another set of steps led down to the building's cellar. No one was supposed to go down here except the janitors. But Robbie, Ethan, Sharon, and Jenna were sitting on the steps, talking and laughing.

"Morganita," Robbie said, using a nickname he had given me in fifth grade. I hadn't heard it for years, and I smiled.

"We were just talking about your birthday," said Jenna.

"Oh!" I said in surprise. "How did you know about it?"

"I told them," said Robbie, drinking from a carton of orange juice. "Let the cat out of the bag."

"Speaking of cats, how's Dagda?" Jenna asked.

Matt's long, black-jean-clad legs obscured my view for a moment as he came and sat on the step above Jenna. She gave him a faint smile but didn't respond when he rubbed her shoulder.

"He's great," I said enthusiastically. "And he's growing really fast!"

"So your birthday's this weekend?" Sharon asked.

"Sunday," I said.

"Let's have a special birthday circle on Saturday, then," said Jenna. "With a cake and all."

Sharon nodded. "That sounds good," she said.

"Um, I can't make it Saturday night," Matt mumbled. He ran a hand through his thick black hair, lowering his eyes.

We all looked at him.

"I've got family stuff to do," he added, but the words were empty.

He is the worst liar in the world, I thought, seeing Jenna staring at him.

"Actually, could we do the birthday thing some other time?" Robbie asked. "I'm thinking I wouldn't mind skipping Saturday night's circle, too."

"Why?" I asked.

"Bree's been after me to come to one of their circles," Robbie admitted. I was surprised by his honesty, not in a bad way—but I felt a renewed rush of anger toward Bree. Robbie shrugged. "I don't want to join their coven, but it wouldn't be a bad idea for me to go to one of their circles, see what they're doing, scope it out."

"Like spying?" Jenna asked, but her tone was soft.

Robbie shrugged again, his hair falling onto his forehead. "I'm curious," he said. "I care about Bree. I want to know what she's doing."

I swallowed and forced myself to nod. "I think that's a good idea," I said. I couldn't believe that Bree would try to poach from our coven, but on the other hand, I was glad that Robbie wanted to keep an eye on her to make sure she wasn't doing anything crazy.

"I don't know," said Cal, shifting and stretching his legs out two steps below. "A lot of what's important in Wicca is continuity. It's about getting in touch with the day-in, day-out stuff, the cycle of the year, the turn of the wheel. Meeting every Saturday, being committed to that, is part of it. It's not something you should skip whenever you want to."

Matt stared at the floor. But Robbie looked back at Cal calmly.

"I hear what you're saying," Robbie said. "And I agree with it. But I'm not doing this just for me, and it isn't just because I feel lazy or I want to watch the game. I need to know what's going on with Bree and her coven, and this is how I can find out."

I was impressed with the air of quiet confidence Robbie projected. His acne and glasses had been gone ever since I'd put a healing spell on him. But something seemed to have healed inside him as well, something that didn't have anything to do with my magick. After years of being a somewhat awkward geek, he was growing into himself and finding new sources of strength. It was great to see.

Cal was silent for a while, and he and Robbie regarded each other. A month ago I would never have thought that Robbie would be a match for someone as strong as Cal, but now they didn't seem that different in a way.

Finally Cal nodded and let out a breath. "Yeah, okay. It won't kill us to take a break. Since there's only seven of us, if two of us can't make it, the circle will be kind of unbalanced. So let's all just take Saturday night off, and we'll meet again the week after."

"And *that's* when we'll have Morgan's birthday cake," said Robbie, smiling at me.

Sharon cleared her throat. "Um . . . I guess this isn't a good time to mention that next Saturday I'll be in Philadelphia for Thanksgiving."

Cal laughed. "Well, we'll just do the best we can. It's always tough around the holidays, with everyone having family stuff. How about you, Matt? Can you make it the following week?"

Matt nodded automatically, and I wondered if he'd even heard what Cal had said. The bell rang, and we all stood. Jenna put her hand in Matt's, staring into his face. He looked drawn, tense. I wished I knew what was going on.

As I headed to homeroom, the halls rapidly filled with streams of students, and Cal tugged on my coat sleeve.

"This Saturday we can have a birthday circle, just us two," he whispered into my ear. "This could be a good thing."

I shivered with delight and looked up at him. "That would be great."

He nodded. "Good. I'll plan something special."

In homeroom I noticed that Tamara was absent. Janice told me she had a cold. Everyone seemed to have colds lately.

Bree was absent, too, or so I thought before I saw her stop outside the class door. She was dressed all in black and was wearing vivid dark makeup, like Raven. It obscured her naturally beautiful face and made her seem anonymous somehow, as if she were wearing a mask. It filled me with an uneasy feeling. She stood outside, talking in a low voice to Chip Newton, and then they both came in and sat down.

I swallowed. Chip was cute and seemed like a pretty nice guy. He was brilliant in math, too—way better than me, and I'm pretty good. But Chip was also our school's biggest dealer. Last year Anita Fleming had gone to the hospital after overdosing on Seconal that she had gotten from him. Which made me wonder just how nice he really was.

What are you doing with him, Bree? I asked silently. And what's your coven up to?

Later that morning, while I was in the first-floor girls' bathroom, I heard Bree's voice, then Raven's, outside my stall. Quickly I pulled up my feet and braced them against my door so nobody could tell that the stall was occupied. I just didn't feel up to facing the two of them, having them sneer at me, right now.

"Where are we meeting?" Raven asked. I heard Bree rustling in her purse, and in my mind's eye I could picture her fishing out lipstick.

"At Sky's place," answered Bree. My interest perked up. They must be talking about their new coven.

"It's so cool that they have their own place," said Raven. "I mean, they're barely older than we are."

I breathed silently, intent on their voices.

"Yeah," said Bree. "What do you think of him?"

"He's hot," said Raven, and they laughed. "But it's Sky who knocks me out. She knows everything, she's so cool, and she's got awesome powers. I want to be just like that." I heard more rustling, then one of them turned on the water for a moment.

"Yeah," said Bree. "Did you think it was weird, what she was talking about on Saturday?"

"Not really," Raven said. "I mean, everything has a light side and a dark side, right? We have to be aware of it."

"Yeah." Bree sounded thoughtful, and I wondered what

the hell Sky had been talking about. Was Sky pulling them toward dark magick? Or was she just showing them part of Wicca's big circle, like Cal had said? It didn't seem—

"You got the hair, didn't you?" Raven asked.

"Yeah," Bree answered. Now she sounded almost . . . depressed. I couldn't follow the conversation at all. What hair?

"What's wrong?" Raven demanded. "Sky promised no one would get hurt."

"I know," Bree mumbled. "It's just, you know, I found the hair in this old comb—"

"Morgan will be *fine,*" Raven interrupted.

"That's not what I was talking about," Bree snapped. "I'm not worried about her."

My eyes flew open wide. I bit my lip to keep from gasping as everything fell into place. Bree was talking about *my* hair. I couldn't believe it. She was turning over a strand of my hair to a strange girl—a witch—behind my back.

There could be only one reason: Sky wanted my hair to put a spell on me. So why had Bree gone through with it? Did she really believe that Sky didn't intend to harm me? Why *else* would she want the hair?

Or did Bree want me to be harmed? I wondered miserably.

"We need more people," Raven stated in the silence.

"Yeah. Well, Robbie's going to come. And we might get Matt, too."

Raven laughed. "Yeah. Matt. Oh God, I can't wait to see Thalia's face when Robbie walks in. She'll probably jump him right there."

I frowned. Who was Thalia?

"Really?" Bree asked.

"She just broke up with her boyfriend, and she's trolling," Raven said. "And Robbie's really hot now. I wouldn't mind hooking up with him myself."

"Oh, Jesus, Raven," said Bree.

Raven laughed again, and I heard a purse being zipped shut. "Just kidding. Maybe."

Silence. I held my breath.

"What?" said Raven as the door opened.

"Thalia's not his type," Bree said as sounds from the outside hall filtered into the room.

"If she wants him, she's his type."

The bathroom door closed again, and air exploded from my lungs. I got to my feet, shaking with reaction. So Sky was manipulating Bree. They were definitely trying to get Matt and Robbie to leave our coven and join theirs. And Sky had her own place, where they were meeting. Did she live with Hunter? Was that who Raven thought was hot? Maybe. Then again, Raven thought most breathing males were hot. And they knew somebody named Thalia who was going to jump Robbie. For some reason, Bree had sounded less than thrilled by that idea—as she had about turning over my hair to Sky. But her reluctant tone was small consolation.

I hated everything that I had just overheard. But more than that, now I was afraid.

10.
Magesight

Things are starting to heat up, and not just because of the Seeker. We have been having many visitors. Many I've never seen before—others I remember from all over the world: Manhattan, New Orleans, California, England, Austria. They come and go at all hours, and I keep coming across little knots of people huddled in this room or that, heads together, discussing, arguing, making magick. I don't know all of what's going on, but it's clear that our discovery here has set many things in motion. And the circles! We are having them almost every day now. They are powerful and exhilarating, but they leave me tired the next day.

    —Sgàth

After school I wanted to talk to Cal about what I had overheard, but he was already gone. He'd left a note on my locker, saying he'd had to go home and meet with one of his mother's friends. So for now I was on my own with my questions about Bree and Raven and their coven. Even Mary K. wasn't coming home with me. As I was getting into Das Boot, she ran up to tell me she was going to Jaycee's house.

I nodded and waved, but I couldn't bring myself to smile. I didn't want to be alone. Too much was troubling me.

Luckily Robbie sauntered over to the car. "What's up?" he asked.

I shielded my eyes from the pale November sunlight and looked at him. I wasn't sure whether or not I should tell him what was on my mind. I decided not to. It was too complicated. Instead I merely said, "I was thinking about going to Butler's Ferry park and gathering some pinecones and stuff for Thanksgiving."

Robbie thought for a moment. "Sounds cool," he said. "Do you want some company?"

"Absolutely," I said, unlocking the passenger-side door.

"So, do you have family coming in for Thanksgiving?" he asked.

I nodded as I pulled out of the driveway, picking up speed on the open road. "My mom's parents, my dad's brother and his family. And then everyone who lives in town. We're having dinner at our house this year."

"Yeah. We're going to my aunt and uncle's," Robbie said without enthusiasm. "They'll be yelling at the football game on TV, the food will suck, and then my dad and Uncle Stan will both get plastered and end up taking a swing at each other."

"Well, they do that every year," I said, trying to inject some humor in a not-so-humorous situation. I'd heard about this from Robbie before, and it always made me sad. "So it's almost, like, traditional."

He laughed as I turned onto Miltown Pike. "I guess you're right. Tradition is a good thing. That's something I've learned from Wicca."

Soon I was pulling into the empty Butler's Ferry parking lot and cutting the engine. I retrieved a basket with a handle from the trunk. Despite the cold the sun was trying hard to shine, and it glittered off the leaves crumpling under our feet. The trees were bare and sculptural, the sky wide and a pale, bleached blue. The peace of the place began to steal over me, calm me down. I felt suddenly happy to be here with Robbie, whom I'd known for so long.

"So are there any herbs or anything around this time of year?" Robbie asked.

"Not a lot." I shook my head. "I checked my field guide, and we might see some stuff, but I'm not counting on it. I'll have to wait till spring. I'll be able to collect plants in the wild then and also start my own garden."

"It's weird that you're so powerful in Wicca, isn't it?" Robbie asked suddenly. But it wasn't a mean or probing question.

For a moment my breath stopped, and I thought about telling him everything that I had learned about myself in the past month. Robbie didn't even know I was adopted. But I just couldn't tell him. He'd been my friend for so long; he'd listened to me complain about my family, and he'd always pictured me as one of them: a Rowlands. I wasn't up to dealing with the emotional backlash of spilling the whole story *again*. I knew I would tell him sometime. We were too close for me to have this huge a secret. But not today.

"Yeah, I guess," I said finally, keeping my voice light. "I mean, it's amazing. But who would've thunk it?"

We grinned at each other, and I found a pretty pine branch on the ground that had three perfect little cones on it. I also stopped to pick up a few oak twigs that had clumps of dried leaves on them. I love the shape of oak leaves.

"It's really changed everything," Robbie murmured, picking up a likely branch and handing it to me. I accepted it, and it joined the others in my basket. "Magick, I mean. It's completely changed your life. And you completely changed my life." He gestured to his face, his skin. I felt a brief stab of guilt. All I'd meant to do was try a tiny healing spell to clear up the acne that had scarred his face since seventh grade. But the spell had continued to perfect him. He didn't even need glasses anymore. Every once in a while the whole thing spooked me all over again.

"I guess it has," I agreed quietly. I leaned down to study a small, fuzzy vine climbing a tree. It had a few withering, bright red leaves on it.

"Don't touch that," said Robbie. "It's poison ivy."

I laughed, startled. "Great witch I'll make." We smiled at each other in the deepening twilight, the silence of the woods all around us. "I'm glad there's no one else besides you here," I added. "I know you won't think I'm a complete idiot."

Robbie nodded, but his smile faded. He bit his lip.

"What's wrong?" I asked.

"Do you miss Bree?" Robbie asked out of the blue.

I stared at him, unable to answer. I didn't know what to say. But I knew what he was feeling: here we were, having fun as we'd done so many times in the past—only Bree wasn't here to share the fun with us.

"I'm in love with her, you know," he said.

My jaw dropped open. Wow. I'd had some suspicions about his feelings for her, but I'd never imagined they were so strong. Nor did I ever expect him just to put them out there like that.

"Uh, I guess I sort of figured you liked her," I admitted awkwardly.

"No, it's more than that," Robbie said. He looked away and tossed an acorn off into the bushes. "I'm in love with her. Crazy about her. I always have been, for years." He smiled and shook his head. I stole a quick glance at him, and any regrets I had about healing his face vanished. I'd done a good thing. He was handsome, secure; his jaw was smooth and strong. He looked like a model.

"Years?" I asked. "I didn't know that."

He shrugged. "I didn't want you to. I didn't want anyone to know, especially Bree. She's always gone for the dumb, good-looking types. I've been watching her be with one jerk after another, knowing I never had a chance." His smile faltered. "You know she told me about when she lost her virginity?" He turned to me, his blue-gray eyes glinting in fading sunlight. He shook his head again, remembered pain on his face. "She was all happy and excited. The best thing since mocha latte, she said. And with that loser, Akers Rowley."

I frowned. "I know. Akers was an ass. I'm sorry, Robbie."

"Anyway," Robbie went on, his smile returning, "have you looked at me lately?"

"You're gorgeous," I said instantly. "You're one of the best-looking guys in school."

Robbie laughed, sounding for a moment like his old awkward and self-conscious self. "Thanks. But, um, do you think maybe I have a shot now?"

I bit my lip. Now, there was a loaded question. I mean, totally apart from the fact that Bree might be getting involved in dark magick, it was so odd to think of her and Robbie as a couple. They'd been friends for so long. "I don't know," I said after a minute. "I don't know how Bree sees you. Yeah, you're good-looking, but she might think of you more as a brother. You sort of know her too well to put a spell on her. Or vice versa." I grinned. "Nonmagickally speaking."

Robbie nodded, kicking his boots through the leaves. His forehead was creased.

We walked deeper into the woods. We had only about twenty minutes before it would be dark; soon we'd have to turn around.

I threaded my arm through his. "There's something else," I said. I felt I needed to warn him, to put him on his guard. "Today I heard Bree and Raven talking about their new coven."

I told him the gist of what I had overheard in the bathroom, leaving out the part about my hair. That was something I had to deal with myself, with Cal's help. Besides, I wasn't even sure what the strand of hair meant. I didn't want Robbie to feel any more torn between me and Bree than he already did. But at the same time I didn't want her to use him.

"Yeah, I know they want to recruit new members," he acknowledged. "Don't worry, I'm not interested. But I am going to go and see what's going on."

Here with Robbie, in the woods, my thoughts about Bree and Raven and their coven began to seem a little paranoid. So what if they wanted to have their own coven? That wasn't necessarily bad or evil. It was just different, another spoke on the wheel. And the hair . . . well, who knew what that was about? Sky had told them no one would get hurt, and they seemed to trust her. But most of all, I just couldn't see Bree as evil. She'd been my best friend for so long. I'd know if there was something really warped about her. Wouldn't I?

I shook my head. It was too hard to think about. Then I remembered something else that I'd overheard. "Do you know someone named Thalia?" I asked Robbie. "She's in Bree and Raven's coven."

He thought and shook his head. "Maybe she's a friend of Raven's."

"Well, my informants tell me she may make a move on you," I said. I'd meant it as a joke, but the words came out sounding dark for some reason.

Robbie brightened. "Excellent," he said.

I laughed and poked him in the side as we walked along the park path.

"Just watch out, okay?" I said after a while. "I mean, with Bree. She tends to like guys she can control, you know? Guys she can intimidate, who'll do whatever she wants. They don't last long."

Robbie was silent. I didn't have to tell him all this; he knew it already.

"If Bree could care about you in the way you deserve," I went on, "it would be great. But I don't want you to get hurt."

"I know," he said.

I squeezed his arm a little tighter. "Good luck," I whispered.

He smiled. "Thanks."

For just a minute I wondered about love spells, love potions, and whether they ever worked. But Robbie broke into my thoughts, as if reading my mind.

"Don't you dare interfere with this magickwise," he warned me.

I feigned a hurt expression. "Of course not! I think I've done enough already. . . ."

Robbie laughed.

Suddenly I stopped short and pulled on his arm. He glanced at me quizzically. I raised a finger to my lips. My eyes scanned the woods. I saw nothing. But my senses . . . there was someone here. Two someones. I could feel them. But where were they?

After another moment I heard muffled voices.

Without thinking, we both dropped down behind a large boulder by the side of the path.

"You're wrong—I don't want to," someone was saying.

My eyes met Robbie's and widened. It was Matt's voice.

"Don't be silly, Matt. Of course you want to. I've seen how you look at me."

Of course. It was Raven—and she was trying to seduce Matt. It made perfect sense. I remembered how she'd said his name in the bathroom, how she'd laughed.

Without speaking, Robbie and I peeked over the top of the boulder. About twenty feet from us Matt and Raven were standing face-to-face. The sun was dropping rapidly now, the air turning colder. Raven moved closer to him, a smile playing on her lips. He frowned and stepped back but bumped into a tree. She moved in and pressed herself against him from chest to knee.

"Stop," he said weakly.

Raven wrapped her hands around his neck and stood on tiptoes to kiss him.

"Stop," he repeated, but the word had about as much force as Dagda's meowing. He resisted for a grand total of five seconds, then his arms went around her, his head slanted, and he pulled her to him tightly. Next to me Robbie dropped his head into his hands. I gaped at them for a little while longer—but when Matt unzipped Raven's coat and unbuttoned his own, I couldn't stand it anymore. Robbie and I leaned with our backs against the boulder. I heard a small moan and cringed. This was too embarrassing.

Robbie leaned closer and breathed into my ear. "Do you think they're gonna do it?"

I grimaced. "I don't know. I mean, it's freezing out here."

Robbie let out a muffled snort. Then I started giggling. For several seconds we crouched low and chewed on our coat sleeves, choking with laughter. Finally Robbie had to look. He eased his head around the boulder into the woods. "I can't see much," he complained in a whisper. "It's too dark in the trees."

I didn't want to look myself, though I knew I could have seen everything clearly. My night vision had improved dramatically; I could see easily in the darkness now, as if everything was illuminated slightly from within. I'd even found a reference to that power in a witchcraft book: it was called magesight.

"I don't think they're doing it," Robbie whispered, squinting.

"It looks more like heavy making out. They're still standing."

"Thank the God and Goddess," I muttered.

I heard Matt's voice: "We have to stop. Jenna . . ."

"Forget Jenna," Raven murmured beguilingly. "I want you. You want me. You want to be with me, in our coven."

"No, I—"

"Matt, please. Quit fighting it. Just give in and you can have me. Don't you want me?"

He gave a strangled moan. Now it was my turn to cover my face with my hands. I wished I could stop Matt somehow. Of course, I was also thinking he was a total jerk.

"You *do* want me," Raven coaxed. "And I can give you what you want. What Jenna can't do for you. We can be together, and we can make magick, strong magick, in my coven. You don't want to be with Cal anymore. He's a control freak."

I stiffened and frowned. What the hell did she know about Cal?

"In our circle you can do what you want," Raven continued. "No one will hold you back. And you can be with me. Come on. . . ."

Raven's voice had never sounded so sweet and pleading. A shiver went down my spine that had nothing to do with the cold.

"I can't," Matt answered. His voice was tortured. We could hear their footsteps in the fallen leaves. Luckily they were moving away from us.

"My ass is frozen," Robbie whispered. "Let's get out of here."

I nodded and stood. As quietly and swiftly as we could, we hurried back down the path to Das Boot. Without a word I dumped my basket of decorations in the trunk, and we hopped into the car.

"That was weird," Robbie finally muttered, blowing on his hands.

I nodded and jammed my key into the ignition. "Now we know why he's being strange," I said as I cranked the heater. I grinned. "Raven's totally hot for him."

Robbie didn't smile, and my own smile faded quickly. This wasn't funny. Not in the least. People could get hurt. I pulled Das Boot out of the parking lot and onto the road.

"Do we do anything about it?" I asked. "I feel sorry for Jenna. I even sort of feel sorry for Matt. He's just . . . lost."

"Do you think Raven's working a spell on him?" Robbie asked.

I shook my head. "I don't know. I mean, she isn't a blood witch. It would be different if she had been doing Wicca for years and was more in touch with her natural power. I don't really see it. Unless Sky did something to her that made her able to do something to Matt . . ."

"I guess it's enough to use the spell of sex," said Robbie dryly.

I thought back to how Cal had made me feel, to the few times we had been close and making out—how swept away I had been, how almost everything faded away except him.

"Yeah," I muttered. "So what do we do?"

Robbie thought. "I don't know. I can't see confronting either of them about it. In a way, it isn't our business. What if you told Cal? I mean, it's his coven they're trying to split up. Tell him the stuff you overheard at school."

I sighed, then nodded. "Good idea." I bit my lip. "Robbie—thanks for telling me about how you feel about Bree. I'm glad you trusted me. And I won't tell anyone else. But just . . . be careful, okay?"

Robbie nodded. "I will."

11.
The Council

Samhain Eve, 1995.

My cousins are having a costume party on Samhain, after we do the service. I'm going as the Dagda, the Lord of the Heavens, and high king of the Tuatha De Danaan. I'm going to carry my panpipes for music, my wand for magick, and a book for knowledge. It'll be fun. I've been helping Linden and Alwyn with their costumes, and we've laughed a lot.

I saw my cousin Athar kissing Dare MacGregor behind a tree in the garden. I teased her and she put a binding spell on me and I can't even tattle. I've been looking for the antispell for two days.

Next year I'll be making my initiation, and then I'll be a witch. The waiting will be over. I've been studying long enough. Seems like all I've done is study, since I came here. Aunt Shelagh is not so bad, but Uncle Beck is a slave driver. And it's even harder because Linden and Alwyn are always hanging onto me, running after me, asking questions that I have a hard time answering. My mind is always spinning, spinning—like a wheel.

But what I think of most, still, is Mum and Dad. Where are they, and why did they leave us? I have lost so much—my family, my trust. The anger never dies. In a year, I'll learn the truth. Another reason I can't wait for my initiation.

—Giomanach

"I tried to call you last night," I told Cal, pressing my face against his warm coat. The chill air swept across the parking lot, rustling my hair. I shivered. His hand stroked my back.

The morning bell was about to ring, but I didn't feel like sharing Cal with the others right now. I didn't want to see Matt and Jenna, either. My nerves felt jangled—both from the bizarre events of yesterday and from the awful dreams I'd had last night. Dreams of a dark cloud, like a swarm of black insects, that was chasing me, suffocating me. I'd woken up sweating and shaking, and I hadn't fallen back asleep until dawn. And then Mary K. had woken me up barely an hour later.

"I know," Cal whispered, kissing my temple. "I got your message. But I got back too late to call you. Was it important? I figured if you really needed me, you'd send a witch message."

I wrapped my arms tightly around his waist. "It was just . . . a bunch of weird stuff I wanted to talk to you about."

"Like what?"

For an instant I hesitated. We were leaning against his car, across the street from school, and it felt almost private. Not private enough, though. I glanced around to make sure we were alone. "Well, first I overheard Raven and Bree talking in the girls' bathroom. They were talking about trying to get Matt and Robbie to join their coven. I think they want to split us up. Sky is their leader. They meet at her place, wherever that is. Then Bree said something about how she found some of my hair to give to Sky. I was kind of . . . freaked out," I confessed. "I mean, what does Sky want with my hair?"

Cal's golden eyes narrowed. "I don't know—but I plan to find out." He took a deep breath. "Don't worry. No one is going to interfere with you, Morgan. Not while I'm around."

I was amazed at how comforting I found his words. I felt like a weight had been lifted from my shoulders.

"There's more," I told him. "Later, Robbie and I were in the park, and we saw Raven and Matt actually making out."

Cal's eyebrows rose. "Oh," he said.

"Yeah. It was totally by accident. Robbie and I were walking around, gathering pinecones and stuff, and we saw Raven practically roping and tying Matt, trying to get him to break up with Jenna and join their coven."

"Man," Cal said, frowning. "So you were right—Matt is acting squirrelly, and now we know why."

"Yep."

A thoughtful expression crossed Cal's face. "And Sky's definitely the leader of their coven? That makes sense since you saw her meeting with Bree and Raven."

I nodded. But I couldn't help wondering . . . if Sky was their leader, then what had she been doing at Cal's house with Selene, participating in one of Selene's circles the night I'd found Maeve's Book of Shadows? Was she some kind of Wiccan spy? Did Selene know Sky had her own coven? Did it even matter? My head was spinning. There was so much I didn't understand, so much I had to find out.

At that moment we heard the distant ringing of the homeroom bell, and we both groaned. Going to classes was not my number-one priority today.

With our arms around each other, we started slogging across the dead brown grass toward school. "Let me think about this," said Cal. "I need to talk to Sky, obviously. But I also need to figure out if I should talk to Raven, or Matt, or both."

I nodded. Part of me felt like a tattler. But mostly I was just relieved that Cal knew. I was thinking about talking to Matt myself, but I felt certain that Cal would take care of anything bigger, like with Sky. As we climbed the stone steps of the back entrance, I squeezed his hand good-bye. Yes, I would have to talk to Matt. He was a friend and still a part of our circle. I owed it to him.

"Matt?" I called down the hall. "Do you have a minute?"

It was after lunch and almost time to head to class. My lack of sleep was starting to catch up with me. My feet were definitely starting to drag. I would have given anything to just go curl up somewhere and take a nap. But this was the first chance I'd had to talk to Matt, and I wasn't going to let it slip.

"What's up, Morgan?" Matt asked. He stood in front of me, his face shuttered and remote, his hands in his pockets.

I took a deep breath, then decided just to get right into it. "I saw you and Raven yesterday," I stated baldly. "In Butler's Ferry park."

Matt's black eyes went wide, and he stared at me. "Uh . . . what are you talking about?"

"Come on," I said patiently. I pulled him over to one side

of the hallway so we could talk without being overheard by the occasional wandering student. I lowered my voice. "I mean, I *saw* you yesterday, with Raven, in the park. I know she's trying to get you to join her coven. I know you're fooling around with her."

"I'm not fooling around with her!" Matt insisted.

I didn't even answer. I just raised my eyebrows.

His gaze fell to the floor. "I mean, it hasn't gotten that far," he mumbled, finally giving in. "Jesus, I don't know what to do."

I shrugged. "Break up with Jenna if you want to go out with Raven," I said.

"But I don't want to go out with Raven," Matt said. "I don't want to join her coven. The thing is . . . I've always thought she was kind of hot, you know?" He shook his head as if to clear it. "Why am I even telling you this?"

A couple of freshman girls passed us. Though they were only two years younger, they seemed a world apart from me. They *were* a world apart. They belonged to the world of school and homework and boys. Mary K.'s world. Not mine.

"Why does she want you to join their coven?" I asked.

"I guess they need more people," Matt answered. He sounded miserable. "A bunch of people started coming, but they all dropped out or were kicked out. A lot of them didn't take it seriously."

"But why *you?*" I pressed.

He sniffed. "I don't think it's really me. I mean, I'm nobody. I'm just a warm body."

"You're also part of our coven," I muttered. Part of me wanted to console him, but the other part wanted to wring his neck. "So what are you going to do?" I asked. I crossed my arms and tried not to look too judgmental.

"I don't know."

I sighed. "Maybe you should talk to Cal about this," I suggested. "Maybe he could help you clarify your thoughts."

Matt didn't look so sure. "Maybe," he said doubtfully. "I'll think about it." He glanced up at me. "Are you going to tell Jenna?"

"No." I shook my head. "But she's not stupid. She knows something's wrong."

He laughed distantly. "Yeah. We've been going out for four years. We know each other so well. But we're not even eighteen yet." With that, he pushed himself off the wall and headed off to his class—without so much as even a backward glance.

I watched him leave, thinking about what he'd said. Did he mean he had gotten tied up with Jenna too early and wanted to date other people? As I pondered it, a short rhyme popped into my mind. I repeated the words quietly.

> *"Help him see the way to go*
> *Help him know the truth to show*
> *He is not the hunter here*
> *Nor yet should he be the deer."*

I shook my head and headed to my own class. What did it mean? I wondered. Who knew? These things didn't come with instructions and commentary.

That afternoon when Mary K. and I got home from school, there was a gray car parked in front of our house. I didn't think anything of it—people parked in front of our house all the time. It was probably one of my mother's clients. So I just followed my sister up the walkway.

"Morgan!"

I wheeled at that voice. Hunter Niall was getting out of the car.

"Who's the dish?" Mary K. asked, arching an eyebrow.

I glared at her. "Go inside," I commanded, my heart kicking up a beat. "I'll deal with it."

Mary K. grinned at me. "Ooh. I can't wait to hear all about *this*." She pounded up the porch steps, stomped the ice off her Doc Martens, and went inside.

"Hello, Morgan," Hunter said, approaching me. How did he manage to make a simple greeting sound menacing? I wondered. His cold seemed to have gotten worse, too. His nose was red, and his voice was very nasal.

"What do you want?" I asked, swallowing. I remembered my bad dream of last night, my overwhelming feelings of being smothered, the dark cloud that had been chasing me.

He coughed. "I want to talk to you."

"About what?" I slung my backpack up onto the porch, not taking my eyes off him. I watched his hands, his mouth, his eyes, anything that he could use to do magick. My pulse was racing; my throat felt tight. I wished hard that Cal would suddenly drive up out of the blue. I considered sending him a message with my thoughts, a witch message—but then I realized I should just turn around and go in. I could handle myself. I didn't even need to talk to Hunter.

But for some reason I just stood there as he strode toward me, cutting across our lawn, leaving black footprints in the half-melted ice. He was close enough now that I could see that his fair skin was completely unblemished and there were a few freckles across the bridge of his strong nose. His eyes were cold and green.

"Let's talk about *you*, Morgan," he said, and he pushed his leather cap farther back on his head. A few tufts of blond hair poked out beneath it. "You don't know what you're doing with Cal." He made this announcement firmly but casually, as if he were simply telling me it was four o'clock and time for tea.

I shook my head, feeling the anger rise. "You don't even know—"

"It's not your fault," he interrupted. "This is all new to you."

The anger welled in the pit of my stomach, turning to rage. What right did he have to be so condescending to me?

Hunter fastened his eyes on mine. "You can't be expected to know about Cal, and his mother, and who they are," he said. "No one blames you," he added.

"No one blames me for what?" I demanded. "What are you talking about? I don't even *know* you. Where do you get off telling me anything about people I know, people I care about?"

He shrugged. His manner was as cold as the air around us. "You're stumbling into something bigger and darker than you could possibly imagine."

Rage turned to sarcasm. Hunter definitely brought out the worst in me. "Oh," I said, trying to sound bored. "Stop, stop, you're scaring me."

His face tightened, and he stepped toward me. My stomach clenched, and adrenaline pumped through my veins. I resisted the urge to turn and bolt into the house.

"Cal's lied to you," Hunter snarled. "He isn't what or

who you think he is. Neither he nor his mother. I'm here to warn you. Don't be stupid. Look at me!" He gestured at his puffy eyes and red nose. "Do you think this is normal? Because it isn't. They're working magick on me—"

"Oh, are you kidding me?" I interrupted. "Are you actually telling me they're plotting against you? Give me a break!"

Who *was* this guy? Did he really think I would believe that Cal and Selene gave him a cold with dark magick? Or was he simply some paranoid nut? Maybe I should feel sorry for him—but I couldn't. All I felt was fury. I wanted to shove him as hard as I could, knock him down and kick him. I had never been so angry, not at my parents, or Bree, not even at Bakker. I spun to go inside.

Hunter darted forward and caught my arm in a painful grip. Feeling trapped, furious, I drew my fingers together and smacked his hand. A jolt of crackly blue light jumped from my hand and shocked him. He released me at once, looking startled.

"So that's it," he whispered, rubbing his hand. He nodded in astonishment. "That's why he wants you."

"Get the hell away from me!" I shouted. "Or do you want me to really hurt you?"

Hunter sneered. "Trying to show me just what a powerful Woodbane you are?"

Time seemed to freeze.

"That's right," he whispered. "I know your secret. I know you're Woodbane."

"You don't know anything," I managed. The words came out in a misty whisper.

"Maeve Riordan," he said, shrugging. "Belwicket. They were all Woodbane. Don't act like you don't know."

"You're lying," I spat, but I felt an awful sensation

bubbling inside me, like a boiling cauldron. I wondered if I was going to throw up.

A flash of surprise crossed his face, instantly replaced with suspicion. "You can't hide it," he said. Now he sounded more irritated than arrogant. "You can't pretend it away. You're Woodbane, Cal is Woodbane, and the two of you are dancing with fire. But it's going to stop. You have a choice, and he does, too. I'm here to make sure you make the right one."

Move, I told my body, my feet. Get inside. Move, dammit! But I couldn't.

"Who are you?" I asked. "Why are you doing this to me?"

"I'm Hunter," he said with a sudden, wolfish grin that made me draw in my breath. He looked feral and dangerous. "The youngest member of the International Council of Witches."

My breath was now coming in shallow gasps, as if I were facing death itself.

"And I'm Cal's brother," he said.

12.
The Future

I thank the God and Goddess for her. What a revelation she is, continually. When I was assigned to her, I had no idea she would be anything but an exercise in power. She has become so much more than that. She is a wild bird: delicate but possessing fierce strength. To move too soon would be to watch her take flight in fear.

For the first time in my life there is a chink in my armor, and it is my love.

—Sgàth

I ran up the ice-crusted steps of our house and threw myself through the door. Somehow I knew Hunter wouldn't follow me. The house was wonderfully warm and cozy, and I almost sobbed with relief as I pounded up the stairs and crashed into my bedroom. I had enough presence of mind to lock my door, and when Mary K. knocked a minute later, I called, "I'll be down in a few minutes."

"Okay," she replied. A moment later her feet padded downstairs.

My head was spinning. The first thing I did was run into the bathroom and examine my face in the mirror. It was me, still the same old me, despite the haunted look in my brown eyes and my shock-whitened face. Was Hunter right? Was I Woodbane?

I threw myself onto my bed and pulled Maeve's Book of Shadows out from under my mattress, then started flipping pages. I'd thumbed through the entries before, reading bits here and there, but mostly I'd been plodding through slowly, savoring every word, letting each spell sink in, deepening my knowledge and my only link to the woman who had given birth to me.

Strangely enough, though, it didn't take me long to find what I was looking for. It was from when Maeve was still writing as Bradhadair. She wrote matter-of-factly: "Despite the Woodbane blood in our veins, the Belwicket clan has resolved to do no evil."

With the force of a wave crashing on a beach, Selene's words came back to me: "I know what it contains, and I wasn't sure you were ready to read it."

Selene knew Maeve had been Woodbane. Suddenly my eyes were drawn to a small volume on my desk—the book about Woodbanes that Alyce at Practical Magick had wanted me to read. So . . . Alyce knew, too? Hunter knew? How did everyone know except *me*? Did Cal know? It didn't seem possible.

Hunter was a liar, though. I could feel the fury gathering within me all over again, like storm clouds. Hunter had also said he was Cal's brother. I thought back. I knew that Cal's father had remarried and that Cal had half siblings in England. But Hunter couldn't be one of them—he and Cal seemed practically the same age.

Lies. All lies.

But why was Hunter here? Had he just decided to come to America and mess with my mind? Maybe he *was* Cal's half brother and he was out to get Cal for some reason. And he was attacking me in order to hurt Cal. He was doing a damn good job of it if that was the case.

The whole thing was giving me a horrible headache. I shut the book and pulled Dagda into my arms, listening to his small, sleepy purr. I stayed there until Mary K. called me to tell me dinner was ready.

The meal was practically inedible: a vegetarian casserole that Mary K. had concocted. I wasn't even hungry, anyway. I needed some answers.

Sidestepping a whispered question from Mary K. about Hunter, I told her I'd help her with the dishes later, then asked my parents if I could go to Cal's. Luckily they said yes.

It started to snow again as I pulled away from the house in Das Boot. Of course I was still upset about everything Hunter had said, but I tried not to let it affect my driving. The wipers pushed snow off the windshield in big arcs, and my brights illuminated thousands of flakes swirling down out of the sky. It was beautiful and silent and lonely.

Woodbane. When I got home tonight, I would read the book Alyce had given me. But first I needed to see Cal.

In the long, U-shaped driveway in front of Cal's house, I saw his gold Explorer and another car—a small, green vehicle

I didn't recognize. I plodded through the surface of the snow-fall, feeling the ice crunch beneath my clogs. The wide stone steps had been shoveled and salted. I hurried up and rang the doorbell.

What would I say if Selene answered the door? The last time I had seen her, I was in her private library, basically stealing a book from her. On the other hand, the book was rightly mine. And she *had* allowed me to keep it.

Several seconds passed. There was no stirring inside, at least none that I could hear. I started to feel cold. Maybe I should have called first, I thought. I rang the doorbell again, then reached out with my senses to see who was home. But the house was a fortress. I received no answer. And then a thought occurred to me: It was spelled, deliberately shut off from magick.

Snowflakes gathered on my long hair, as if I wore a lace mantle that was slowly melting against my cheeks and eyelids. I rang again, beginning to feel unsure. Maybe they were busy. Maybe they were meeting with someone. Maybe they were having a circle or working magick or throwing a party . . . but at last the tall, heavy wooden door opened.

"Morgan!" Cal said. "I didn't even feel you come up. You look frozen. Come on in." He ushered me into the foyer and brushed his hand down my cold, damp hair. Light footsteps behind him made me pull back, and I looked up to see Sky Eventide.

I blinked, looking at her. Her face was closed, and I won-dered what I had interrupted. Had Cal invited her here to ask her about her coven and my hair? I glanced at him for signs of irritation or wariness, but he seemed easy and comfortable.

"I should have called," I said, looking from Cal to Sky. "I didn't mean to interrupt anything."

Tell me what I'm interrupting, I thought as Sky reached for her heavy leather coat. She looked beautiful and exotic. Next to her I felt about as exciting as a brown field mouse. I had a tingle of jealousy. Did Cal find her attractive?

"It's all right," Sky said, zipping her coat. "I was just leaving." Her black eyes searched Cal's and held them. "Remember what I said," she told him, ignoring me. The words seemed to have an element of threat, but Cal laughed.

"You worry too much. Relax," he said cheerfully, and she just looked at him.

I watched as she opened the front door and left, not bothering to say good-bye. There was something strange going on here, and I needed to know what it was.

"What was all that about?" I asked point-blank.

Cal shook his head, still smiling. "I ran into her earlier and told her I wanted to talk to her about what she's up to with her coven. So she came over—but all she wanted was to be Hunter's messenger," he said, tugging on my coat so it came off. He draped it over a high-backed chair and then took my hand, rubbing its coldness away. "Hey, I tried to call you a few minutes ago, but the phone was busy."

"Someone must be on-line," I guessed, frowning. Was he trying to change the subject? "What kind of message did Sky have?"

"She was warning me," he answered simply. Still holding my hand, he led me through a pair of dark wooden doors that opened into a large, formal parlor. A fire was blazing in an enormous stone hearth, and in front of it a deep blue sofa beckoned. Cal sat and pulled me down to sit next to him.

"Warning you?" I pressed.

He sighed. "Hunter's out to get me, basically, and Sky was telling me to be on my guard. That's all."

I frowned into the fire. Usually I felt reassured by the heat and glow of flames—but not now. "Why is Hunter out to get you?"

Cal hesitated. "It's . . . um, kind of personal," he said.

"But why was Sky warning you? Isn't she with him?"

"Sky doesn't know what she wants," Cal answered cryptically. He hadn't shaved in a while, and the shadow of stubble across his face made him look older. Sexier, too. He was quiet for a few moments, and then he edged closer to me, so I felt his warmth from my shoulder to my hip. A memory swept over me: of how it had felt to lie next to him, to kiss him deeply, to have his hands touch me and to touch him back. But I couldn't allow myself to be distracted.

"Who *is* Hunter?" I asked.

Cal made a face. "I don't want to talk about him," he said.

"Well, he came to see me today."

"What?" Shock flared in Cal's golden eyes. I saw something else there, too. Concern, maybe. Concern for *me*.

"What's the International Council of Witches?" I pressed on.

Cal drew away from me, then sighed in resignation. He sat back against the couch and nodded. "You'd better just tell me everything," he said.

"Hunter came to my house and said I was Woodbane," I said. The words flowed from my mouth as if a dam had been broken. "He said *you* were Woodbane and that he was your brother. He said I was stumbling into danger. He said he was on the International Council of Witches."

"I can't believe this." Cal groaned. "I'm sorry. I'll make sure he leaves you alone from now on." He paused, as if collecting his thoughts. "Anyway, the International Council of Witches is just what it sounds like. Witches from all over the world getting together. It's kind of a governing body, though what they govern isn't really clear. They're kind of like village elders, but the village consists of all witches everywhere. I think there's something like sixty-seven countries represented."

"What do they do?"

"In the old days they often settled disputes about land, clan wars, cases of magick being used against others," Cal explained. "Now they mostly try to set guidelines about appropriate use of magick, and they try to consolidate magickal knowledge."

I shook my head, not quite understanding. "And Hunter's part of it?"

Cal shrugged. "He says he is. I think he's lying, but who knows? Maybe the council is really hard up for members." He gave a short laugh. "Mostly he's just a second-rate witch with delusions of grandeur."

"Delusions is right," I murmured, remembering how Hunter had claimed his cold was the result of a spell. That was so obviously ridiculous that maybe I should just forget about everything else he'd said, too. But somehow I couldn't.

Cal glanced at me. "He told you that you were Woodbane?"

"Yes," I said stiffly. "And I went inside and found it in Maeve's BOS. I *am* Woodbane. All of Belwicket was. Did you know?"

Cal didn't answer right away. Instead he seemed to weigh my words. He looked at the fire. "How do you feel about that?" he finally asked.

"Bad," I said honestly. "I would have been really proud to be Rowanwand or even anything else. But to be Woodbane . . . it's like finding out my ancestors are a long line of jailbirds and lowlifes. Worse, really. Much worse."

Cal laughed again. He turned to me. "No, it's not, my love. It's not that bad."

"How can you say that?"

"It's easy," he said with a grin. "Nowadays it isn't a big deal. Like I said, people have sort of a prejudiced view of Woodbanes, but they're ignoring all their good qualities, like strength, and loyalty, and power, and pursuit of knowledge."

I stared at him. "You didn't know I was a Woodbane? I'm sure your mom does."

Cal shook his head. "No, I didn't know. I haven't read Maeve's book, and Mom didn't discuss it with me. Listen, knowing you're Woodbane isn't a bad thing. It's better than not knowing your clan at all. Better than being a mongrel. I've always thought the Woodbanes have gotten a bad rap— you know, revisionist history."

I turned back to the fire. "He said you were Woodbane, too," I whispered.

"We don't know what we are," Cal said quietly. "Mom has done a lot of research, but it isn't clear. But if we were, would it matter to you? Would you not love me?"

"Of course it wouldn't matter," I said. The flames crackled with life before us, and I rested my head on Cal's shoulder. As upset as I had been, I was starting to feel better. I kicked off my shoes and stretched my feet out to the fire. My socks hung loose. The heat felt delicious on my toes, and I sighed. I still had more questions to ask.

"Why did Hunter say he was your brother?"

Cal's eyes darkened. "Because my dad's a high priest and very powerful. Hunter wants to be that way, too. And he *is* the son of the woman my father married after he left my mom. So we're at least stepbrothers."

I swallowed, wincing. "Ouch," I murmured. "I'm sorry."

"Yeah. Me too. I wish I'd never met him."

"How did you meet?" I asked cautiously.

"At a convention, two years ago," Cal answered.

I was startled into laughter. "A witch convention?"

"Uh-huh," said Cal, smiling a little. "I met Hunter, and he informed me we were only six months apart and brothers. Which would mean that my father had deliberately gotten another woman pregnant while my mom was pregnant with *me*. I hated Hunter for that. I still don't want to believe it. So no matter what Hunter says, I say that his father is someone else, not my dad. I can't accept that my father, total jerk that he is, would have done that." He put his arm around me, and I rested my chin on his chest, hearing the steady thumping of his heart, sleepily watching the fire.

"Is that why Hunter is acting this way?"

"Yeah, I think so. Somehow he's all . . . I don't know, bent and twisted. It must have something to do with his childhood. I know I shouldn't hate him—it's not his fault my dad's life is so messy. But he just—got off on telling me that my dad fathered him. Like he enjoyed hurting me."

I gently stroked Cal's wavy hair. "I'm sorry," I said again.

Cal gave a rueful chuckle, and I wanted to comfort him, the way he had comforted me so many times. Gently, I kissed him, trying to give him love he could be sure of. He almost purred with contentment and held me closer.

"Why was Hunter here, in your mother's house, that night when she had the circle?" I asked softly when I stopped for breath.

"He likes to keep in touch with us," Cal said sarcastically. "I don't know why. Sometimes I think he likes Mom and me to just remember he's alive, that he exists. Rubbing our faces in it, I guess."

I shuddered. "Ugh. He's horrible. I don't feel the least bit sorry for him. I just can't stand him—and I hate what he's doing to you. If he keeps on, he'd better watch out."

Cal grinned. "Mmmm, I like it when you talk tough."

"I'm serious," I told him. "I'll zap him with witch fire so hard, he won't know what hit him." I flexed my fingers, surprised at the violence of my own feelings.

Cal's smile broadened, but he said, "Look, let's just change the subject." He kissed me, then pulled away. "I have a question for you. What are you thinking about in terms of college?"

I furrowed my brow, surprised and bemused. "I'm not sure," I said. "For a while I thought I'd apply to MIT or maybe Cal Tech. You know, something for math."

"Brain," Cal teased affectionately.

"Why do you want to know?" I asked. It seemed so oddly normal, coming right after all this talk about a Council of Witches and ancient magickal clans.

"I've been thinking about our future," he said. His tone was very straightforward, relaxed. "I was thinking about going to Europe next year, maybe taking a year off to travel. I was also thinking, maybe I could get us a little place when I come back and we could both go to the same school."

My eyes widened with shock. "You mean . . . *live together?*" I whispered.

"Yes, live together," he said, flashing me a little half grin as if he were talking about doing our homework together or going to see a movie. "I want to be with you." He drew back and looked deeply in my eyes. "No one's ever wanted to protect me before, like you do."

My breath came fast at the thought. Laughing, I grabbed him, knocking him back on the sofa. I meant to kiss him, but we ended up toppling onto the floor with a thud.

"Ow," said Cal, rubbing his head. He smiled at me and I kissed him. But right at that moment I caught a glimpse of an old grandfather clock. My spirits sank. It was getting late. Mom and Dad would start to worry.

"I have to go," I said reluctantly.

"Someday you won't have to," he promised.

Then I was getting into my coat, melting with happiness, and Cal was walking me out. I didn't even feel the cold until I was almost home.

13.
Dark Side

Litha, 1996

Until now my life has been winter. But last night, at my initiation, spring broke through the ice. It was magick. Aunt Shelagh and Uncle Beck led the rite. The coven elders gathered around. I was blindfolded and given wine to drink. I was tested and I answered as best I could. In my blindness I made a circle and drew my runes and cast my spells. The warmth of the summer night fled before the cold draughts of the North Sea, blowing off the coast. Someone held the sharp point of a dagger to my right eye and told me to step forward. I tried to remember if I'd seen any coven members with ruined eyes, and I couldn't, so I stepped smartly forward, and the sharp tip faded away.

I sang my song of initiation alone, in the darkness, with the weight of the magick pressing in on me, and my feet stumbling in the rough heathers of the headland. I sang my song, and the magick came to me and lifted me up, and I felt huge and powerful and bursting with joy and knowledge. Then I was unblindfolded and the initiation was complete. I was a witch and a full-grown man in the eyes of the craft. We drank wine and I hugged everyone. Even Uncle Beck, and he hugged me back and told me he was proud of me. Cousin Athar teased me but I just grinned at her. Later I hunted Molly F. down and gave her a real kiss, and she pushed me away and threatened to tell Aunt Shelagh.

I guess I wasn't as much of a man as I thought.

—Giomanach

On Friday when I woke up, the remnants of disturbing dreams fluttered in my mind like torn banners. I stretched several times, trying to snap myself out of it—and then they faded, and I had no idea what they'd been: there were no lingering images or clear emotions to give me a clue. I just knew they'd been bad.

I had stayed up too late the night before, reading both Maeve's Book of Shadows and the book about Woodbanes that Alyce had given to me. It was still very strange for me, knowing Maeve was my birth mother and now knowing she was also Woodbane. Throughout my entire life I had felt just a bit different from my family, and I had wondered why. The odd thing was, now that I knew my origins, I felt more like a Rowlands and less like an Irish witch.

I could tell it was cold and disgusting outside just from looking out the window. And I was snug in my bed, and I had beside me a small kitten who was completely adorable and sound asleep.

So there was no way I was getting up.

"Morgan, you have to hurry!" Mary K. shouted, sounding frantic. A second later she burst into my room and tugged at my comforter. "We have ten minutes to get to school, and it's snowing and I can't ride my bike. Come on!"

Damn, I thought, giving in. One day I would really have to act on my desire to skip school.

We made it just as the late bell rang, and I skittered into class just as my name was called for roll.

"Here!" I said unnecessarily, panting and sliding into my seat. As Tamara smirked at me, I pulled out my brush and began untangling my hair. Across the room Bree sat talking to Chip Newton. I thought about Sky and Raven and their coven, about Sky telling them about the dark side. I still didn't have a clear idea of what the dark side was except for some vague paragraphs in one of my Wicca books. I would have to do more research. I would have to finish reading the book Alyce had given me about the Woodbanes. Cal had said there was no dark side per se, there was only the circle of Wicca. Maybe I should ask Alyce about it.

I glanced over at Bree, as if looking at her would tell me what she was doing or thinking. I used to be able to look in her eyes and know exactly what was going on with her—and also tell her exactly what was going on with me. Not anymore. We spoke different languages now.

It was an odd day.

At school Matt wouldn't meet my eyes. Jenna seemed nervous. Cal was fine, of course; we both knew we had reached a new level of closeness. We'd made plans for the future. Every time we saw each other, we smiled. He was a ray of light to me. Robbie was his usual comforting self, and it was interesting to see how girls who'd never noticed him before were now going out of their way to talk to him, to walk next to him, to pepper him with questions about homework and chess problems and what kind of music he liked. Ethan and Sharon were still circling each other flirtatiously.

Yet the whole day I felt on edge somehow. I hadn't gotten enough sleep, and I had too many questions ricocheting around my brain. I couldn't relax and pay attention in class. In my mind I kept going over what I had read in Maeve's book. Then my thoughts would flash to Hunter's bizarre behavior—and then to lying with Cal in front of the fire at his house, feeling so full of love for him. Why couldn't I focus? I needed to be alone or, better yet, with Cal—to meditate and focus my energy.

After school I waited for Cal by his car. He was talking to Matt, and I wondered what they were saying. Matt looked uncomfortable, but he was nodding. Cal seemed to be making him feel better. That was good. But I also hoped he was letting Matt know that it was very uncool to mess around with Raven behind Jenna's back.

Finally Cal saw me. He strolled right over and put his arms around me, pinning me to his car. I was aware of Nell Norton walking by, looking envious, and I enjoyed it.

"What are you up to right now?" I asked. "Can you hang out?"

"I wish I could," he said, holding a handful of hair and kissing my forehead. "Mom has some people in from out of town, and she wants me to meet with them. People from her old coven in Manhattan."

"How many covens has she had?" I asked, curious.

"Hmmm, let's see," Cal said, counting under his breath. "Eight, I think. She forms a coven in a new place and makes sure they're really strong, then she trains a new leader, and when they're ready, she moves on." He smiled down at me. "She's like the Johnny Appleseed of Wicca."

I laughed. Cal kissed me again and got into his car, and I headed for Das Boot. A minivan slowed next to me, and the window went down. "Going home with Jaycee!" Mary K. called. She waved, and I waved back. I saw Robbie pull away in his car, and down the block Bree climbed into her BMW and drove off. I wished I knew where she was going but didn't have the emotional or physical energy to follow her.

Instead I headed for Red Kill.

Practical Magick smelled like steam and tea and candles burning. I stepped in and felt myself relax for the first time since I had pried myself out of bed this morning.

For a moment I stood just inside the door, warming up, feeling my chest expand and my fingers thaw. My hair was slightly damp from the snow, and I shook it out so it would dry. David looked up from the checkout counter and regarded me with his full attention. He didn't smile but somehow he conveyed the impression of being glad to see me. Maybe I was finally used to him, because it felt like see-ing an old friend. I hadn't felt an immediate connection with him as I had with Alyce, and I wasn't sure why. But maybe I was getting over it.

"Hello, Morgan," he said. "How are you?"

I thought for a moment, then shook my head with a tired smile. "I don't know."

David nodded, then stepped through a curtained door in back of the counter, revealing a small, cluttered room. I saw a tiny, battered table with three chairs, a rusty apartment-size fridge, and a two-burner hot plate. A teakettle was already starting to whistle there. Strange, I thought. Had he somehow known I was coming?

"You look like you could use some tea," he called.

"Tea would be great," I said sincerely, deciding to accept the friendship he seemed to be offering. "Thanks." I stuffed my gloves into my pockets and looked around the store. No one else was here. "Slow day?" I asked.

"We had some people in this morning," David replied from behind the curtain. "But it's been quiet this afternoon. I like it this way."

I wondered if they made any money doing this.

"Um, who owns this store?" I asked.

"My aunt Rose, actually," said David. "But she's very old now, and doesn't come in much anymore. I've been working here for years—on and off since right after college." I heard some clinking of spoons in mugs, and then he ducked back through the curtain, carrying two steaming cups. He handed one to me. I took it gratefully, inhaling its unusual fragrance.

"Thanks. What kind of tea is this?"

David grinned and sipped his own. "You tell me."

I looked at him uncertainly, and he just waited. Was this a test? Feeling self-conscious, I closed my eyes and sniffed deeply. The tea had several scents: they blended together into a sweet whole, and I couldn't identify any of them.

"I don't know," I said.

"You do," David encouraged quietly. "Just listen to it."

Once again I closed my eyes and inhaled, and this time I let go of the knowledge that this was tea in a mug. I focused on the odor, on the qualities carried by the water's steam. Slowly I breathed in and out, stilling my thoughts, relaxing my tension. The more still I became, the more I felt part of the tea. In my mind's eye I saw the gentle steam rising and swaying before me, dissolving in the slightest breath of air.

Speak to me, I thought. Show me your nature.

Then, as I watched inside my mind, the steam coiled and separated into four streams, like a fine thread unraveling. With my next breath I was alone in a meadow. It was sunny and warm, and I reached out to touch a perfect, rounded pink blossom. Its heavy aroma tickled my nose and bathed me in its beauty.

"Rose," I whispered.

David was quiet.

I turned to the next steam thread and followed it, saw it being dug from the ground, black dirt clinging to its rough skin. It was washed and peeled, and when its pink flesh was grated, a sharp tang was released.

"Oh, ginger," I listed, nodding.

The third strand drifted from rows and rows of low-growing, silver-green plants covered with purple flowers. More bees than I had ever seen buzzed over the plants, creating a vibrant, living mantle of insects. Hot sun, black earth, and the incessant drone filled me with a drowsy contentment.

"Lavender."

The last thread was a woodier scent, less familiar and also less pretty. It was a low-growing, crinkle-leafed plant, with slender stalks of miniature flowers. I crushed some of the leaves in my hand and smelled them. It was earthy and different, almost unpleasant. But intertwined with the other three scents, it made a beautifully balanced whole: it added strength to their sweetness and tempered the pungent odor of the ginger.

"I want to say skullcap," I said tentatively. "But I'm not sure what that is."

I opened my eyes to find David watching me.

"Very good," he said with a nod. "Very good indeed. Skullcap is a perennial. Its flowering stems help diminish tension."

By now the tea had cooled a bit, and I took a sip. I didn't notice the actual flavors so much; I was more aware of drinking the different essences, allowing them to warm me and infuse me with their qualities of healing, soothing, and calming. I perched on a stool next to the counter. But then, without warning, all the unsettled aspects of my life crept up and made me feel like I was suffocating again. Matt and Jenna, Sky and Bree and Raven, Hunter, being Woodbane, Mary K. and Bakker . . . it was overwhelming. The only thing that was going right was Cal.

"Sometimes I feel like I don't know anything," I heard myself blurt out. "I just want things to be straightforward. But things and people have all these different layers. As soon as you learn one, then another pops up, and you have to start all over again."

"The more you learn, the more you need to learn,"

David agreed calmly. "That's what life is. That's what Wicca is. That's what you are."

I looked at him. "What do you mean?"

"You thought you knew yourself, and then you found out one thing and then another thing. It changes the whole way you see yourself and see others in relation to you." He sounded very matter-of-fact.

"You mean, *one* does these things or me in particular?" I asked carefully.

Outside, the weak afternoon sun gave up its struggle and faded behind a bank of gray clouds. I could make out the hulking shape of Das Boot, parked in front of the store entrance, and I saw that it was already covered by at least an inch of snow and tiny rocks of ice.

"Everyone is like that," he said with a smile, "but I was speaking of you in particular."

I blinked, not quite understanding. David had once said that I was a witch who pretended not to be a witch.

"Do you still think I pretend that I'm not a witch?" I asked.

He didn't seem concerned that I knew what he had said. "No." He hesitated, forming his thoughts. He looked up at me, his dark eyes steady. "It's more that you don't present yourself clearly because you aren't yet sure who you are, *what* you are. I've known I'm a witch my whole life— thirty-two years. And I've also always known—" He paused again, as if making up his mind. Then he said quietly, "I'm a Burnhide. It's not only who I am, it's what I am. I'm the same thing on the inside as I am on the outside. You're different in that you've only recently discovered—"

"That I'm Woodbane?" I interrupted.

He gazed at me. "I was about to say, discovered you're a witch at all. But now you know you're Woodbane. You've hardly begun to discover what this means to you, so it's almost impossible for you to project what it should mean to others."

I nodded. He was beginning to make sense. "Alyce once told me that you and she were both blood witches, but you didn't know your clans. But you're a Burnhide?"

"Yes. The Burnhides settled mostly in Germany. My family was from there. We've always been Burnhides. Among most blood witches your clan is considered a private matter. So many people lost all knowledge of their house that nowadays most people say they don't know their clan until they know someone well enough."

I felt pleased that he had trusted me. "Well, I'm Woodbane," I said awkwardly.

David grinned without prejudice. "It's good to know what you are," he said. "The more you know, the more you know."

I laughed at that and drank my tea.

"Are there any ways to really identify the clans?" I asked after a moment. "I read that Leapvaughns tend to have red hair."

"It's not incredibly reliable," David answered. The phone rang, and he cocked his head for a moment, concentrating, then didn't answer it. In the back room I heard the answering machine pick it up.

"For example, lots of Burnhides have dark eyes, and lots of them tend to go gray early." He gestured to his own silvery hair. "But that doesn't mean every dark-eyed, gray-haired person is a Burnhide nor that all Burnhides look like this."

I had a sudden thought. "What about this?" I asked, and

pulled up my shirt to show him the birthmark on my side, under my right arm. My need to know outweighed my embarrassment.

"Yeah, the Woodbane athame," David said matter-of-factly. "Same thing. Not all of you have them."

It was somehow shocking to hear so casually that I had been marked this way my whole life, marked with the symbol of a clan, and that I had never known.

"What about . . . the International Council of Witches?" I asked, my brain following a series of thoughts.

The brass bells over the door jangled, and two girls about my age came in. Without deliberately deciding to, I sent out my senses and picked up the fact that they seemed nonmagickal: just girls. They walked through the store slowly, whispering and laughing, looking at all the merchandise.

"It's an independent council," David said softly. "It's designed to represent all the modern clans—there are hundreds and hundreds who aren't affiliated with any of the seven houses. Its main function is to monitor and sometimes punish the illegitimate use of magick . . . magick used to gain power over others, for example, or to interfere with others without their knowledge or agreement. Magick used to harm."

I frowned. "So they're sort of like the Wicca police."

David raised his eyebrows. "There are those who see the council that way, certainly."

"How do they know if someone is using magick for the wrong reasons?" I asked. Behind us the girls had left the book aisle and were now oohing and aahing over the many beautiful handmade candles the store stocked. I waited to hear them come across the penis-shaped candles.

"Oh my God," whispered one, and I grinned.

"There are witches within the council who specifically look for people like that," David explained. "We call them Seekers. It's their job to investigate claims of dark magick or misuse of power."

"Seekers?" I said.

"Yeah. Wait a second. I can tell you more about them." David ducked out from the counter and headed down the book aisle. He paused for a moment in front of a shelf, then chose an old, worn volume and pulled it out. He was already thumbing through pages when he got back to me. "Here," he said. "Listen to this."

I stared at him as he began to read, sipping my tea.

"'I am sad to say that there are those who do not agree with the wisdom and purpose of the High Council. Some clans exist who wish to remain separate, secretive, and insulated from their peers. Certainly no one could fault a clan for guarding private knowledge. We all agree that a clan's spells, history, and rituals are their province alone. But we have seen in these modern times that it is wise to join together, to share as much as we can, to create a society in which we can fully participate and celebrate with others of our own kind. This is the purpose of the International Community of Witches.'"

He paused for a moment and glanced at me.

"That sounds like a good thing," I said.

"Yes," he said, but there was an odd tone in his voice. His eyes flashed back down to the page. "'One cannot help but question those who refuse to participate, who work against this goal and use magick that the council has decried.

In the past such apostasy was the undoing of countless numbers. There is little strength in being alone and little joy in unsanctified magick. That is why we have Seekers.'"

There was something about the way he said *seekers* that gave me a chill. "And what do they do, exactly?" I pressed.

"'Seekers are council members who have been selected to find witches who have strayed beyond our bounds,'" he continued. "'If they discover witches who are actively working against the council, working to harm themselves or others, then they have been given license to take action against them. It is better that we police our own, from within, before the rest of the world chooses once again to police us from without.'" David closed the book and looked at me again. "Those are the words of Birgit Fallon O'Roark. She was high priestess of the High Council from the 1820s to the 1860s."

My tea was starting to get cold. I finished it all in a big gulp and placed the mug on the counter. "What do the Seekers do if they find the witches working against the council?" I asked.

"Usually they put binding spells on them," said David, looking troubled. His voice sounded strained, as if the words themselves were painful to say. "So they can't use their magick anymore. There are things you can do, certain herbs or minerals that you can make them ingest . . . and they can no longer get in touch with their inner magick."

A cold wind seemed to pass over me. My stomach twisted. "Is that bad?" I asked.

"It's very bad," said David emphatically. "To be magickal and not be able to use your magick—it's like suffocating. Like being buried alive. It's enough to make someone lose their mind."

I thought of Maeve and Angus, living in America for years, renouncing their powers. How had they borne it? What had it done to them? I thought about my suffocating dream—how intolerable it had been. Was that what their everyday life had been like for them without Wicca?

"But if you're abusing your power, a Seeker will come for you sooner or later," said David, shaking his head, almost as if to himself. His face seemed older, lined with memories I didn't think I wanted to know about.

"Hmmm." Outside it was dark. I wondered who Cal was meeting and if he would call me later. I wondered if Hunter was really from the council. He seemed more like one of the bad witches the council would send a Seeker to track down.

I wondered if Maeve and the rest of Belwicket had been successful in renouncing the dark side. Would the dark side allow itself to be renounced?

"Is there a dark side?" I said the words tentatively, and felt David draw back.

"Oh, yes," he said softly. "Yes, there's a dark side."

I swallowed, thinking of Cal. "Someone told me there was no dark side—that all of Wicca was a circle and everything was connected to each other, all part of the same thing. That would mean there aren't two different sides, like light and dark."

"That's true, too." David sounded thoughtful. "We say bright and dark when talking about magick used for good and magick used for bad, or evil—to give it a common name."

"So they're two different things?" I pressed.

Slowly David ran his finger around the circular rim of his cup. "Yes. They are different but not opposite. Often they're right next to each other, very similar. It has to do with philosophy and how people interpret actions. It has to do with the spirit of the magick, with will and intent." He glanced up at me and smiled. "It's very complicated. That's why we have to study our whole lifetimes."

"But can you say that someone is on the dark side and that they're evil and you should stay away from them?"

Again David looked troubled. "You could. But it wouldn't be the whole picture. Are there witches who use magick for the wrong purposes? Yes. Are there witches who deliberately hurt others for their own gain? Yes. Should some witches be stopped? Yes. But it usually isn't that simple."

It seemed that nothing in Wicca was simple, I thought. "Well, I'd better get home," I said, pushing my mug across the counter. "Thanks for the talk. And for the tea."

"It was my pleasure," said David. "Please come back any time you need to talk. Sometimes Alyce and I . . . feel concerned about you."

"Me?" I asked. "Why?"

A slight smile turned up the corners of David's mouth. "Because you're in the middle of becoming who you will be," he said gently. "It isn't going to be easy. You may need help. So feel free to ask us for it."

"Thanks," I said again, feeling reassured but still not quite understanding what he meant. With a little wave I left the warmth of Practical Magick and went out to my car. My tires slid a tiny bit as I backed up, but soon I was on the road heading back to Widow's Vale, my headlights illuminating each unique, magickal snowflake.

14.
Scry

Litha, 1996

Early this morning Uncle Beck and I sat on the edge of the cliff and watched the sun come up, my first sunrise as a witch, and he told me the truth about Mum and Dad. In all the years since they disappeared, I have fought back tears at every turn, telling myself not to give in to childish grief.

But today the tears came, and it's strange, because now I am supposed to be a man. Still, I wept. I wept for them, but mostly for me—for all the anger I have wasted. I know now that Uncle Beck had good reasons for keeping the truth from me, that Mum and Dad had to disappear in order to protect me, Linden, and Alwyn. That he's heard from them only once, two years ago. That he hasn't even ever tried to scry for them.

And I know why.

And now I also know what to do with myself, where I'm

going, what I'll be, and it's funny, because it's all in my name anyway. I am going to hunt down those who ripped my family apart, and I won't stop until I draw Yr on their faces with their blood.

    —Giomanach

I was barely two miles from my house when I saw the headlights behind me. First there was nothing, not another car in sight. Then I rounded a corner, and suddenly the lights were right there in my rearview mirror, blinding me, filling my car as if it were lit from within. I squinted and flashed my brakes a few times, but whoever it was didn't pass or turn off the brights. The headlights drew closer.

I slowed Das Boot, sending the message of "get off my tail," but the other car glued itself to my bumper, tailgating me. Mild road rage started to build. Who could be following me like this? Some practical joker, a jerk kid with his dad's car? I jammed my foot on the gas, but the car sped up as I did. The tires skidded slightly as I rounded another corner. The car matched my movement. A prickle of nervousness shot down my spine. My wipers were click-clicking away—matching my pulse—clearing away the falling snow. I couldn't see any other lights on the road. We were alone.

Okay. Something was definitely wrong. I'd heard stories about car jackers . . . but I was in a '71 Valiant. No matter how much I loved it, I doubted anyone would try to steal it from me by force, especially not in the middle of a snowstorm. So what was this idiot doing?

My eyes shot to the rearview mirror. The headlights

bored into my pupils. I blinked, trying to clear my vision of a sea of purple dots. Anger began to turn to fear. I could barely see a thing in the darkness . . . nothing except those lights, the lights that seemed to grow in strength with each passing second. But for some reason, I couldn't hear the other car's engine. It was as if—

Magick.

The word slithered into my thoughts like a snake.

I bit my lip. Maybe that wasn't a car behind me at all. Maybe those two lights were some manifestation of a magickal force. I had a sudden, vivid memory of Hunter Niall peering under Cal's Explorer, of Cal showing me that rune-inscribed stone. We knew Hunter had tried to use magick on us once already. What if he was doing it again now, to me?

Home, I thought. I just needed to get home. I flipped up my mirror so the light wouldn't blind me. But there was about another mile and a half of road until I made it to my street. That was actually pretty far. "Crap," I muttered, and my voice shook a little. With my right hand I drew signs on my dashboard: Eolh, for protection; Ur, for strength; and Rad, for travel. . . .

The lights seemed to flash even brighter in my mirror. My left hand jerked involuntarily on the steering wheel. All at once I felt something bumpy under my wheels.

Before I knew it, I was sliding sideways out of control into the deep drainage ditch. *Goddess!* I screamed silently. Fear and adrenaline pierced my body, a slew of invisible arrows. My hands gripped the steering wheel. I had lost control; the tires screeched. Das Boot lurched sideways on an ice slick, like a heavy white glacier.

The next few seconds unfolded in slow motion. With a sickening crunch the car's nose rammed a pile of ice and snow. I jerked forward and heard the shattering of a headlight. Then silence. The car was no longer moving. But for a few seconds I sat there—paralyzed, unable to move. I was conscious only of my own breathing. It came in quick, uneven gasps.

All right, I finally said to myself. I'm not hurt.

When I lifted my head, I thought I saw the briefest flash of two red taillights, vanishing into the night.

My eyes narrowed. So . . . it *had* been a real car after all.

With a trembling sigh I turned off the engine. Then I threw open the door and hoisted myself out of the driver's seat—no easy feat, considering Das Boot was skewed at a crazy angle. It was hard to concentrate, but I called on my magesight and peered down the road in the direction that the car had disappeared. All I saw, though, were trees, sleeping birds, the faint glow of living nocturnal creatures.

The car was gone.

I leaned against my door, breathing hard, my fists clenched inside my pockets. Even though I was pretty sure those lights hadn't been magickal, the fear didn't subside. Somebody had run me off the road. Das Boot was hopelessly lodged in the ditch. A lump formed in my throat. I was on the verge of bursting into tears, shaking like a leaf. What was going on? I remembered the runes I had drawn on the dash right before the wreck, and now I redrew them in the chill air around me. Eolh, Ur, Rad. The brisk movement helped calm me slightly, at least enough for me to try to figure out what to do.

Actually, there was pretty much only one option. I had to walk the rest of the way home. I didn't have a cell phone, so

I couldn't call anyone for help. And I didn't exactly feel like waiting around in the darkness on this frozen, lonely road all by myself.

Heaving open the driver's door again, I fished inside for my backpack and carefully locked Das Boot. I shook my head. It was going to be a long, miserable march to my house. But as I heaved the backpack across my shoulder, a flash of dim light illuminated the snowflakes around me, and I heard the faint rumble of a motor. I turned to see a car slowly approaching . . . from the same direction the lights had vanished.

The flash of relief I'd briefly felt at the possibility of being rescued evaporated as the car rolled to a stop, not fifteen feet from where I stood. The headlights weren't nearly as bright, but for all I knew, this was the same car. Maybe the person driving had decided to turn around and finish me off, or—

My insides clenched. The license plate, the grating of the tan BMW . . . I recognized it even before the passenger window unrolled. It was Bree's car.

Bree looked across from the driver's seat, her eyes outlined in black, her skin pale and perfect. We regarded each other silently for a few moments. I hoped I didn't look as freaked out and disheveled as I felt. I wanted to radiate strength.

"What happened, Morgan?" she asked.

I opened my mouth, then closed it. My eyes narrowed as a horrible thought struck me. Could Bree have been the one who'd run me into the ditch?

It was possible. There were no other cars on the road. She could have made a U-turn up ahead and come back to see what had happened to me. But . . . Bree? Hurt me?

Remember what you heard in the bathroom, a voice

inside chimed. She gave your hair to a witch. Remember.

Maybe things had changed permanently. Maybe Bree no longer cared about me at all. Or maybe Sky Eventide had put her up to this—as a stunt to scare me, the same way that Sky had forced her to turn over a lock of my hair. A thousand thoughts pounded against my skull, aching to be let out, to be heard: Oh God, Bree, don't let them fool you! I'm worried about you. I miss you. You're being so stupid. I'm sorry. I need to talk to you. Don't you know what's happened to me? I'm adopted. I'm a blood witch. I'm Woodbane. I'm sorry about Cal—

"Morgan?" she prodded, her brow furrowed.

I cleared my throat. "I hit a patch of ice," I said. I gestured unnecessarily to Das Boot.

"Are you okay?" she asked stiffly. "Did you hurt yourself?"

I shook my head. "I'm fine."

She blinked. "Do you want a ride home?"

I took a deep breath but shook my head again. I couldn't get into her car. Not when she might have been the one who had run me off the road in the first place. Even though I could hardly believe I was having such horrible thoughts about someone who had once been my best friend, I didn't dare risk it.

"Are you sure?" she pressed.

"I'll be fine," I mumbled.

Without another word she rolled up her window and took off. I noticed that she accelerated slowly so she wouldn't splatter me with snow and slush.

My chest ached as I walked home.

My parents fussed over me, which was nice. I told them I'd skidded off the road on a bad patch of ice, which was true in a way, but I left out the part about the other car behind me. I didn't want to worry them any more than necessary. I called a tow truck company, who agreed to get Das Boot and bring it home later that night. Thank the Goddess for Triple A, I thought and decided to ask for a cell phone for Christmas.

"Are you sure you don't want to come for Chinese with us?" Mom asked, after making sure I had thawed. My parents were heading out to meet Aunt Eileen and Paula, to drive by several houses that were for sale in the area, then to get dinner. They wouldn't be back till late. Mary K. was at Jaycee's, and I was sure she was meeting Bakker later.

"No, thanks," I said. "I'll just wait for the tow truck."

Mom kissed me. "I am so thankful you're okay. You could've been hurt so easily," she said, and I hugged her back. It was true, I realized. I really could have been hurt. If it had happened at another section of the road, I could have gone into a thirty-foot ravine. An image popped into my mind of Das Boot tumbling down a rocky cliff, then bursting into flames—and I cringed.

After Mom and Dad left, I set a pot of water on to boil for frozen ravioli. I grabbed a Diet Coke, and the phone rang. I knew it was Cal.

"Hello there," he said. "We're taking a little break. What are you doing?"

"Fixing some dinner." It was incredible: I still felt a little shaky, even though the mere sound of Cal's voice worked wonders. "I, um, had a little accident."

"What?" His voice was sharp with concern. "Are you okay?"

"It wasn't anything," I said bravely. "I just went off the road and ended up in a ditch. I'm waiting for the tow truck to bring Das Boot home."

"Really? Why didn't you call me?"

I smiled, feeling much better as I dumped a bunch of ravioli into the water. "I guess I was still recovering. I'm okay, though. I didn't hurt anything except my car. And I knew you were busy, anyway."

He was quiet for a moment. "Next time something happens, call me right away," he said.

I laughed. If it had been anyone else, I would have said they were overreacting. "I'll try not to do it again," I said.

"I wish I could come see you," he said, sounding frustrated. "But we're doing a circle here and it's about to start. Lousy timing. I'm sorry."

"It's fine. Don't worry so much." I sighed and stirred the pot. "You know, I . . ." I left the sentence hanging. I was going to tell him about seeing Bree, about all of my terrible fears and suspicions, but I didn't. I couldn't bear to reopen the wound, to allow all those painful emotions to come flooding back.

"You what?" Cal asked.

"Nothing," I murmured.

"You're sure?"

"Yeah."

He sighed, too. "Well, okay. I should probably go. My mom is starting to do her stuff. I'm not sure how late this will go—I might not be able to call you later. And you know we don't pick up the phone if it rings during a circle, so you won't be able to call me."

"That's okay," I said. "I'll see you tomorrow."

"Oh, tomorrow," said Cal, sounding brighter. "The famous pre-birthday day. Yeah, I have special plans for tomorrow."

I laughed, wondering what plans he had made. Then he made a silly kissing noise into the phone, and we hung up.

Alone and quiet, I ate my dinner. It felt soothing to be by myself and not have to talk. In the living room I noticed a basket full of fatwood by the fireplace. In just a few minutes I had a good blaze going, and I fetched Maeve's BOS from upstairs and settled on the couch. My mom's one crocheting attempt had resulted in an incredibly ugly afghan the size and weight of a dead mule. I pulled it over me. Within moments Dagda had scrambled up the side of the couch and was stomping happily across my knees, purring hard and kneading me with his sharp little paws.

"Hey, cute thing," I said, scratching him behind his ears. He settled on my lap, and I started reading.

July 6, 1977

Tonight I'm going to scry with fire. My witch sight is good, and the magick is strong. I used water once, but it was hard to see anything. I told Angus and he laughed at me, saying that I was a clumsy girl and might have splashed some of the water out of the glass. I know he was teasing, but I never used it again.

Fire is different. Fire opens doors I never knew were there.

Fire.

The word rolled around my head, and I glanced up from the page. My birth mother was right. Fire *was* different. I'd loved fire since I was little: its warmth, the mesmerizing golden red glow of the flames. I even loved the noise fire made as it ate the dry wood. To me it had sounded like laughter—both exciting and frightening in its hungry appetite and eager destruction.

My eyes wandered to the burning logs. I shifted carefully on the couch, trying not to disturb Dagda, though he could probably sleep through almost anything. Facing the flames, I let my head rest against the back of the couch. I set the BOS aside. I was one hundred percent comfortable.

I decided to try to scry.

First I released all the thoughts circling my brain, one by one. Bree, looking at me standing in the snow by the side of the road. Hunter. His face was hard to get rid of—and when I pictured it, I got angry. Over and over I saw him, silhouetted against a leaden gray sky, his green eyes looking like reflections of Irish fields, his arrogance coming off him in waves.

My eyelids fluttered shut. I breathed in and out slowly. The tension drained from each muscle in my body. As I felt myself drift more completely into a delicious concentration, I became more and more aware of my surroundings: Dagda's small heart beating quickly as he slept, the ecstatic joy of the fire as it consumed the wood.

I opened my eyes.

The fire had transformed into a mirror.

There in the flames I saw my own face, looking back: the long sweep of brown hair, the kitten in my lap.

What do you want to know? the fire whispered to me. Its voice was raspy and sibilant—seductive yet fleeting, fading away in acrid curls of smoke.

I don't understand anything, I answered. My face was

serene, but my silent voice cried out in frustration. *I don't understand anything.*

Then in the fire a curtain of flame was drawn back. I saw Cal, walking through a field of wheat as golden as his eyes. He swept out his hand, looking beautiful and godlike, and it felt like he was offering the entire field to me as a gift. Then Hunter and Sky came up behind him, hand in hand. Their pale, bleached elegance was beautiful in its own way, but I felt a terrible sense of danger suddenly. I closed my eyes as if that might blot it out.

When I opened them again, I found myself walking through a forest so thickly grown that barely any light reached the ground. My bare feet were silent on the rotting leaves. Soon I saw figures standing in the woods, hidden among the trees. One of them was Sky again, and she turned and smiled at me, her white-blond hair glowing like an angel's halo around her. Then she turned to the person behind her: it was Raven, dressed all in black. Sky leaned over and kissed Raven gently, and I blinked in surprise.

Many disjointed images flowed over each other next, sliding across my consciousness, hard to follow. Robbie kissing Bree . . . my parents watching me walk away, tears running down their faces . . . Aunt Eileen holding a baby.

And then, as if that movie were over and a new reel began, I saw a small, white clapboard house, set back on a slight rise among the trees. Curtains fluttered from the open windows. A neat, tended garden of holly bushes and mums lined the front of the house.

Off to one side was Maeve Riordan. My birth mother.

I drew in my breath. I remembered her from another

vision I'd had, a vision of her holding me when I was an infant. She smiled and beckoned to me, looking young and goofy in her 1980s clothes. Behind her was a large square garden of herbs and vegetables, bursting with health. She turned and headed toward the house. I followed her— around the side, where a narrow walk separated the house from the lawn. Turning to face me again, she knelt and gestured underneath the house, pointing.

Confusion came over me. What was this? Then a phone began ringing from far away. Although I tried to keep concentrating, the scene began to fade, and my last image was of my birth mother, impossibly young and lovely, waving good-bye.

I blinked, my breathing ragged.

The sound of a phone still filled my ears. What was going on? Several seconds passed before I realized that it was *our* phone, not a phone in my vision. The images were all gone now. I was alone in our house again—and somebody was calling.

15.
Presence

September 4, 1998

Uncle Beck hit me last night. Today I have a shiner and a split lip. It looks really impressive, and I'm going to tell people I got it defending what's left of Athar's honor.

Two years ago, on the dawn after my initiation, Uncle Beck told me why Mum and Dad disappeared. How Mum had seen the dark cloud coming when she was scrying, and how it had nearly killed her, right through the vision. And how, right after they escaped and went into hiding, their coven was wiped out. I remember all the witches in the coven, how they were like aunts and uncles to me. Then they were dead, and Linden and Alwyn and I came to live with Beck and Shelagh and Athar and Maris and Siobhan.

Since then I've been trying to find out about the dark wave, the force of evil that destroyed my parents' coven and made them go into hiding. I know it's got something to do with Woodbanes. Dad is—or was—Woodbane. The last time I was in London, I went to all the old bookshops where they sell occult books. I visited the Circle of Morath, where they keep a lot of the old writings. I've been reading and searching for two years. Finally last night, Linden and I were going to try to call on the dark side, to get information. Since Linden's initiation last month, he's been pestering me to let him help, and I had to say yes, because they were his parents too. Maybe in two years, when Alwyn's initiated, she'll want to work with us. I don't know.

Anyway, Uncle Beck found us in the marshes a mile from the house. We hadn't even got far in the rite, and suddenly Uncle was storming up, looking huge and terrible and furious. He broke through our circles, kicked out our candles and our fire, and knocked the athame from my hand. I've never seen him so angry, and he hauled me up by my collar as if I was a dog and not sixteen and as tall as him.

"Call on the blackness, will you?" he growled, while Linden jumped to his feet. "You bloody bastard! For eight years I've fed you and taught you and you've slept under my roof, and you're out here dealing with blackness and leading your young brother astray?" Then he punched me, knocked me down, and I hit the ground like an unstrung puppet. The man has a fist like a ham—only harder.

We had words, we thrashed it out, and at the end, he understood what I wanted, and I understood that he'd rather *kill me than let me do it, and that if I involved Linden again I would need to find another place to live. He's a good man, my uncle, and a good witch, though we often clash. Mum is his sister and I know now that he desires to right the wrong done to her as much as I. The difference is that I was willing to cross the line to do it, and Beck isn't.*

—Giomanach

"Hello?" I said into the receiver. I realized that I had no sense of who it was, even though I usually did before I picked up the phone.

Silence.

"Hello?" I said again.

Click. Drone of dial tone.

Okay, I knew, of course, that people get wrong numbers all the time. But for some reason, maybe because I was still caught up in images, emotions, and sensations from the fire, this silent phone call unnerved me. Every spooky movie I had ever seen came back to haunt me: *Scream, Halloween, The Exorcist, Fatal Attraction, Blair Witch*. My only thought was: Someone was checking to see if I was home. And I was. Alone.

I punched in star sixty-nine. Nothing happened. Finally a computerized female voice told me that the number I was trying to reach was blocked.

Feeling tense, I slammed the phone down on the hook. Then I began to race around the house, locking the front and back doors, the basement door, locking windows that had never been locked in my memory. Was I being stupid? It didn't matter. Better stupid and safe than smart and dead. I turned on all the outside lights instead of just the dim yellow glow of the front porch fixture.

I didn't know why I felt so afraid, but my first sense of alarm was rapidly growing into pure terror. So I retrieved my trusty baseball bat from the mudroom, locked that door, scooped up Dagda, and scampered upstairs to my room, glancing over my shoulder. Maybe it was still the aftermath of the accident, but my hands were clammy. My breath came quickly. I locked my bedroom door, then locked the door that led from the bathroom to Mary K.'s room.

I sat down on my bed, clenching and unclenching my fists. Cal, was all I could think. Cal, help me. I need you. Come to me.

I sent the witch message out into the night. Cal would get it. Cal would save me.

But the minutes ticked by, and he didn't come. He didn't even call to say he was on his way. I thought about calling him, but then I remembered what he'd said about not answering the phone during the circle.

Didn't he get my message? I wondered frantically. Where is he?

I tried to calm myself down. Mom and Dad would be home soon. So would Mary K. Anyway, it was just a phone call. A wrong number. Maybe it was Bree calling to apologize, and she'd lost her nerve.

But why would Bree's number have been blocked? It could have been anyone, though: a prank call by some pimply sixth grader whose mom caught him just before he spoke. Or maybe it was a telemarketer. . . .

Calm down, calm down, I ordered myself. Breathe.

A faint prickling at the edge of my senses made me sit up straight. I cast out my senses, searching as hard as I could. Then I knew what it was. Someone was on the edge of the property. Fear oozed through me like burning lava.

"Wait here," I whispered idiotically to Dagda.

I crept soundlessly to my darkened window and peered out into the yard. As I looked out, the outside lights all blinked off. *Shit.* Who had gotten to them?

I could make out the leaves of the shrubs, the swooping shadow of an owl, the crusts of ice hanging on our fence.

That was when I saw them: two dark figures.

I squinted, using my magesight to make out their features, but for some reason I couldn't focus on their faces. It didn't matter, though. For a moment the night's cloud cover broke and allowed the not quite half-moon to appear. The glint of moonlight reflected off pale, shining hair, and I knew who was here. Sky Eventide. The person with her wore a dark knit cap and was too tall to be either Bree or Raven. Hunter. I felt sure it was Hunter.

Where was Cal?

I watched from my crouching position on the floor as they faded into the house's shadows. When I could no longer see them, I closed my eyes and tried to follow them with my senses. I felt them moving around the perimeter of the house slowly, pausing here and there. Would they try to come in? My fingers tightened on the bat, even though I knew it would be of zero use against witches in full possession of their powers. And Sky and Hunter were blood witches.

What did they want? What were they doing?

And then it came to me: of course. They were putting a spell on my house, on me. I remembered reading about how Maeve and her mother, Mackenna Riordan, had put spells on people. They had often needed to walk around a house or a person or a place. To surround something with magick is to change it.

Sky and Hunter were surrounding *me*.

They were circling my house, and I couldn't stop them— I didn't even have any idea what they were doing. It must have been one of them who had called earlier, to make sure I was home. And maybe they had blocked my call to Cal somehow. He might not be coming at all. . . .

I looked at Dagda to see if he was nervous or upset, if his senses had picked up on the vibrations of danger and magick.

He was asleep: tiny mouth slightly open, blue eyes shut, ribby little side rising and falling with sleep-slowed breaths. So much for the power of animals. I scowled, then looked out the window again. The shadowy figures were no longer visible but still present. Feeling terribly alone, I sat on my floor and waited. It was all I could do.

Three times Hunter and Sky moved around the house. I heard nothing and saw nothing, but I sensed them. They were there.

Almost half an hour later they left. I felt them leave, felt them close a circle behind them . . . felt them send one last line of magick out toward the house and toward me. Soon after that I heard the quiet purr of an engine as it faded down the street. The outside lights all flickered back on. But there was no way I was going outside to see what they had done. No. I was going to stay put.

With my baseball bat at my side, I went back downstairs and watched television until the tow truck driver showed up with Das Boot. Mom and Dad came home a few minutes later. I hurried upstairs to my room before they walked through the front door. I was too wrung out to act normal around them.

Cal never came.

"Hi, honey," Mom said when I stumbled into the kitchen the next morning. "Sleep well?"

"Uh-huh," I said, moving purposefully toward the refrigerator for a Diet Coke. But I was lying. The truth was, I hadn't slept well at all. I'd dozed fitfully, my fleeting dreams filled with images from the fire and the silhouettes of Sky and whoever else had been on our lawn. Finally I'd given up on sleep altogether. I glanced at the kitchen clock. Only eight-thirty. I wanted to call Cal, but it was too early, especially for a Saturday morning.

"Does anyone have plans for today?" Dad asked, folding back the newspaper.

"Jaycee and I are going to Northgate Mall," said Mary K. She fiddled with a box of Pop-Tarts, still in her pajamas. "The pre-Thanksgiving sales are starting."

"I'm going to be getting ready for tomorrow," said Mom. She flashed a meaningful smile at me. "Morgan, do you want an ice-cream cake this year?"

Suddenly I remembered that the next day was my birthday. Wow. Until this year I'd always eagerly looked forward to my birthday, anticipating it for months and months. Of course, until this year I'd had no idea that I was an adopted blood witch from the Woodbane clan. Nor, in previous years, was I being stalked by other witches. Things had changed a little.

I nodded and sipped my Diet Coke. "Chocolate cake on the bottom, mint-chip ice cream on top," I instructed, summoning up a smile.

"And what do you want for dinner tomorrow night?" Mom asked, starting to make a list.

"Lamb chops, mint jelly, roasted potatoes, fresh peas, salad," I rattled off. The same birthday dinner I always wanted. It was comforting somehow. This was my house, my family, and we were going to celebrate my birthday—same as always.

"Are you going to be busy tonight?" Mom asked, averting her eyes. She knew we usually had circles on Saturday nights.

"I'm seeing Cal," I said.

She nodded and thankfully left it at that.

As soon as I was dressed, I went outside and walked around the house. As far as I could tell, I couldn't feel the effects of a spell's magick. Which could very well be *part* of the spell, of course. Slowly I circled our entire house. I saw no sign of anything. No hexes spray painted on the house, no dead animals hanging from trees. Then again, I knew the signs would be infinitely more subtle than that.

Weirdly enough, even the snow-covered ground betrayed no footprints, though it hadn't snowed since before my visitors had arrived. I searched and searched but saw no trace of anyone's having been in our yard at all—except me, just now. Frowning, I shook my head. Had it all been an illusion? Had it been part of my scrying? How much could I trust my own perceptions? But I remembered the images I had seen—so clearly, too—the sights, sounds, and smells that had accompanied my fire scrying.

Most of all I remembered Maeve, standing by her house, smiling and pointing.

Maeve had lived in Meshomah Falls, two hours away. I glanced at my watch, then went inside to call Cal.

"What happened to your car?" Robbie asked half an hour later. We were in the front seat of Das Boot; I had just picked him up. Thankfully the car still worked, although the right headlight had been shattered and there was a massive dent in the front bumper. When I had called Cal, he hadn't been home—Selene had said he was out shopping, and she wasn't sure when he'd be back. Somehow, speaking to Selene calmed me down. I thought of asking her if he'd gotten my witch message, but my mom was in the room and I didn't want to bring it up in front of her. I'd ask Cal later.

Fortunately Robbie had been home, and he was a happy second choice for the road trip I had planned.

"I went into a ditch last night," I said with a grimace. "Slid on the ice." I didn't mention the lights I'd seen. That was something I'd only talk to Cal about. Whatever was going on, I didn't want to drag Robbie into it.

"Man," said Robbie. "Were you hurt?"

"No. But I have to get my headlight fixed. Big pain."

Robbie opened a map across the dashboard as I pulled away from his house. The day was rapidly clearing: I had a hope of actual sunshine before too long. It was still cold, but the snow and ice were melting slowly, and the streets were wet, the gutters running with water.

"You're looking for a town called Meshomah Falls. It should be north, right up the Hudson," I told him, turning onto the road that would lead to the highway. "About two, two and a half hours away."

"Oh, okay," he said, tracing his finger over the map. "I see it. Yeah, take Route 9 north until we get to Hookbridge Falls."

After a quick stop for gas and a supply of junk food, we were on our way. Bree and I used to go on road trips all the time: just day trips to malls or cool places to hike or little artists' colonies. We had felt so free, so unstoppable. But I tried not to dredge up those memories. Now they just filled me with pain.

"Want a chip?" Robbie offered, and I dug a hand into the bag.

"Have you talked to Bree yet?" I asked, unable to tear my mind from her. "About how you feel?"

He shook his head. "I've sort of tried, but it hasn't actually come up. I guess I'm a coward."

"No, you're not," I said. "But she can be hard to approach."

He shrugged. "You know, Bree asks about you, too," he said.

"What do you mean?"

"I mean, you always ask about her. Well, she asks about you, too. I mean, she never says anything nice about you, you both say mean things about the other one, but even a total idiot could tell that you two miss each other."

My face felt stiff as I stared out the window.

"Just thought you should know," he added.

We didn't say another word for the next sixty miles—not until we saw a sign for the Hookbridge Falls exit. By then the sky had cleared, and it was open and blue in a way it hadn't been for what seemed like weeks. The sun's warmth on my face lifted my spirits. I felt like we were on a real adventure.

Robbie consulted the map. "We get off here and head east on Pedersen, which leads right into Meshomah Falls," he said.

"Okay."

A few minutes after we'd turned off the highway, I saw the sign announcing Meshomah Falls, New York.

A shiver ran down my spine. This was where I had been born.

I drove down Main Street slowly, staring at the buildings. Meshomah Falls was a lot like Widow's Vale, except not quite as old and not quite as Victorian. It was a cute town, though, and I could see why Maeve and Angus had decided to settle here. I picked a side street at random and turned onto it, slowing even more as I looked carefully at each house. Next to me, Robbie chewed gum and drummed his fingers along to the radio.

"So, when are you going to tell me why we're here?" he joked.

"Uh . . ." I didn't know what to say. I guess I had been planning to pass this off as a simple joyride, just a chance to get out and do something. But Robbie knew me too well. "I'll tell you later," I whispered, feeling unsure and vulnerable. To tell him one part of the story would mean telling him everything—and I had yet to come fully to terms with that.

"Have you ever been here before?" Robbie asked.

I shook my head. Most of the houses were pretty modest, but none was immediately recognizable as the house I'd seen in my vision. And they were fewer and farther between now;

we were heading into the country again. I started to wonder what the hell I was doing. Why on earth did I think I'd be able to recognize Maeve's house? And if by some miracle I found it, what would I do then? This whole idea was stupid—

There it was.

I slammed on the brakes. Das Boot squealed to an abrupt halt. Robbie glared at me. But I hardly noticed. The house from my vision, my birth mother's house, stood right before my eyes.

16.
Hidden

January 12, 1999

I've been ill, apparently.

Aunt Shelagh says I have been out for six days. Raving, she told me, with a high fever. I feel like death itself. I don't even remember what happened to me. And no one will say a word. I don't understand any of it.

Where is Linden? I want to see my brother. When I awoke this morning, eight witches from Vinneag were around my bed, working healing rites. I heard Athar and Alwyn in the hall, sobbing. But when I asked if they could come in to see me, the Vinneag witches just gave each other grave glances, then shook their heads. Why? Am I that ill? Or is it something else? What is happening? I must know, but no one will tell me a thing, and I am as weak as a hollow bone.

—Giomanach

The house was on the right side of the road, and as I glanced through Robbie's window, it was as if a cool breeze suddenly washed across my face. I pulled up alongside it.

The walls were no longer white but painted a pale coffee color with dark red accents. The neat garden in front was gone, as was the large herb and vegetable patch to one side. Instead some clumpy rhododendrons hid the front windows on the first floor.

I sat there in silence, drinking in the sight of the place. This was it. This was Maeve's house, and my home for the first seven months of my life. Robbie watched me, not saying anything. There were no cars in the driveway, no sign that anyone was home. I didn't know what to do. But after several minutes I turned to Robbie and took a deep breath.

"I have something to tell you," I began.

He nodded, a somber expression on his face.

"I'm a blood witch, like Cal said a couple of weeks ago. But my parents aren't. I was adopted."

Robbie's eyes widened, but he said nothing

"I was adopted when I was about eight months old. My birth mother was a blood witch from Ireland. Her name was Maeve Riordan, and she lived in that house." I gestured out the window. "Her coven was wiped out in Ireland, and she and my biological father escaped to America and settled here. When they did, they swore never to use magick again."

I took another deep, shaky breath. This whole story sounded like a movie of the week. A bad one. But Robbie nodded encouragingly.

"Anyway," I went on, "they had me, and then something happened—I don't know what—and my mother gave me up for adoption. Right after that, she and my father were locked in a barn and burned to death."

Robbie blinked. His face turned slightly pale. "Jesus," he muttered, rubbing his chin. "And who was your dad?"

"His name was Angus Bramson. He was a witch, too, from the same coven in Ireland. I don't think they were married." I sighed. "So that's why I'm so strong in Wicca, why that spell I did for you worked, why I channel so much energy at circles. It's because I come from a line of witches that's hundreds or thousands of years old."

For what seemed like a long time Robbie just stared at me. "This is mind-blowing," he mumbled finally.

"Tell me about it."

He offered a sympathetic smile. "I'll bet things have been crazy at your house lately."

I laughed. "Yeah, you could say that. We were all freaked out about it. I mean, my parents never told me, not in sixteen years, that I was adopted. And all my relatives knew and all their friends. I was . . . really angry."

"I'll bet," Robbie murmured.

"And they knew how my birth parents died and that witchcraft was involved, so they're really upset that I'm doing Wicca because the whole thing scares them. They don't want anything to happen to me."

Robbie chewed his lip, looking concerned. "No one knows why your birth parents were killed? They were murdered, right? I mean, it wasn't suicide or some ritual gone wrong."

"No. Apparently the barn door was locked from the outside. But they must have been scared about something because they gave me up for adoption right before they died. I can't find out why it happened, though, or who could have done it. I have

Maeve's Book of Shadows, and she says that after they came to America, they didn't practice magick at all—"

"How did you get your birth mother's Book of Shadows?" he interrupted.

I sighed again. "It's a long story, but Selene Belltower had it, and I found it. It was all a bunch of weird coincidences."

Robbie raised his eyebrows. "I thought there weren't any coincidences."

I looked at him, startled. You're absolutely right, I thought.

"So why are we here?" he asked.

I hesitated. "Last night I had a dream . . . I mean, I had a vision. Actually, I scryed in the fire last night."

"You scryed?" Robbie shifted in his seat. Creases lined his forehead. "You mean you tried to divine information, like magickal information?"

"Yes," I admitted, staring down at my lap for a moment. "I know, you think I'm doing stuff I shouldn't be doing yet. But I think it's allowed. It's not a real spell or anything."

Robbie remained silent.

I shook my head and glanced out the window again. "Anyway, I was watching the fire last night, and I saw all sorts of weird images and scenes and stuff. But the most realistic scene, the clearest one, was about this house. I saw Maeve standing outside it and pointing underneath it. Pointing and smiling. Like she wanted to show me something underneath this house—"

"Wait a second," Robbie cut in. "Let me get this straight. You had a vision, so now we're here, and you want to crawl under that house?"

I almost laughed. It didn't sound bizarre; it sounded utterly insane. "Well, when you put it that way . . ."

He shook his head, but he was smiling, too. "Are you sure this is the house?"

I nodded.

He didn't say anything.

"So do you think I'm crazy, coming here?" I asked. "Do you think we should turn around and go home?"

He hesitated. "No," he said finally. "If you had that vision while you were actually scrying, then I think it makes sense to check it out. I mean, if you actually want to crawl under there." He glanced at me. "Or . . . do you want *me* to crawl under there?"

I smiled at him and patted his arm. "Thanks. That's really sweet. But no. I guess I'd better do it. Even though I have no idea what I'm looking for."

Robbie turned to the house again. "Got a flashlight?"

"Of course not." I smirked. "That would make me too well prepared, wouldn't it?"

He laughed as I slid out of the car and zipped up my coat. I hesitated only a moment before I unlatched the chain-link gate, then headed up the walk. Under my breath I whispered: "I am invisible, I am invisible, I am invisible," just in case anyone was watching from one of the neighboring houses. It was a trick Cal had told me about, but I'd never tried it before. I hoped it worked.

On the left side of the house, past the shaggy rhododendrons, I found the place where Maeve had been standing in my vision. There was an opening between the low brick foundation and the floor supports. The opening was barely twenty inches high. I glanced back at the car. Robbie was leaning against it in case he suddenly needed to come to my aid. I smiled and gave him a thumbs-up. He smiled back reassuringly. I was lucky. He was a good friend.

Crouching down, I peered underneath the house and saw only a dense, inky blackness. My heart was pounding loudly, but my senses picked up no people above or around me. For all I knew, I would find dead bodies and crumbling bones in there. Or rats. I would freak if I came face to face with a rat. I pictured myself screaming and scrambling to get out from under the house as fast as I could. But there was no sense in waiting. My magesight would guide me. I crept forward on my hands and knees. As soon as I had edged under the house, I paused to give my eyes time to adjust.

I saw a lot of junk, glowing faintly with time: old insulation foam, an ancient, dirt-encrusted sink, old pipes and chunks of sheet metal. I maneuvered my way carefully through this maze, looking around, trying to get some idea of what I could be looking *for*. I could feel the cold dampness seep through my jeans. I sneezed. It was dank under here. Dank and musty.

Again the questions festered in my mind. Why was I here? Why had Maeve wanted me to come here? Think, think! Could there be something about the house itself? I glanced upward to see if runes or sigils were traced on the bottom of the floor supports. The wood was old and dirty and blackened, and I saw nothing. I swept my gaze from side to side, starting to feel incredibly stupid—

Wait. There was something. . . . I blinked, rapidly. About fifteen feet in front of me, next to a brick piling, there was something. Something magickal. Whatever it was, I could sense it more than I could see it. I crawled forward, ducking low under water pipes and phone wires. At one point I had to shimmy on my belly beneath a sewer line. I was going to look like hell when I got out of here—I could feel my hair dragging in the dirt and cursed myself for not tying it up.

Finally I slithered out and could crawl normally again. I sneezed and wiped my nose on my sleeve. There! Tucked between two supports, practically hidden behind the piling, was a box. In order to get to it, I had to stretch my arms around the piling; the supports blocked my path.

Tentatively I reached for it. The air around the box felt thick, like clear Jell-O. My fingertips pushed through it and reached icy cold metal. Gritting my teeth, I tried to pry it out of the dirt. But it wouldn't budge. And in my awkward position I couldn't get any leverage to give it a good wrench. Again I yanked at it, scratching my fingers on its rusted, pitted surface. There was no use, though. It was stuck.

I felt like screaming. Here I was, on my hands and knees in the mud, under a strange house, *drawn* here—and I was helpless. I leaned forward and squinted at the box, concentrating hard. There, carved into the lid and barely visible under years of dust, were the initials M. R. Maeve Riordan. To me they were as clear as if I were seeing them in sunlight.

My breath came fast. This was it. This was why my mother had sent me here. I was meant to have it—this box that had remained hidden for almost seventeen years.

A memory suddenly flashed through my mind: that day not so long ago, right when we had all first discovered Wicca, when a leaf had fallen on Raven's head and I'd willed it to hover there with my thoughts. It had been nothing more than a flight of whimsy and a gesture of defiance against her for being cruel to me. But now it took on a deeper significance. If I could move a leaf, could I move something heavier?

I closed my eyes, focusing my concentration. Again I

stretched forward and touched the dusty box with my fingertips. My mind emptied, all my thoughts vanishing like
water down a drain. Only one thought remained: What had
once belonged to my birth mother now belonged to me.
The box was mine. I would have it.

It jumped into my hands.

My eyes flew open. A smile crossed my face. I'd done it!
By the Goddess, I'd done it! Clutching the box under one
arm, I scrambled out of there as fast as I could. Outside, the
sunlight seemed overly bright, the air too cold. I blinked and
stood, my muscles cramped, then stamped my feet and
brushed off my coat as best I could. Then I hurried forward.

A middle-aged man was walking up the sidewalk toward the
house. He dragged a fat dachshund behind him by a leash. As he
caught sight of me coming around from the back of the house, he
slowed and then stopped. His eyes were sharp with suspicion.

I froze for an instant, my heart thumping. I am invisible, I
am invisible, I am invisible. I hurled the thought at him with
as much force as I could.

A moment later his gaze seemed to lose its focus. His
eyes slid aside, and he began walking again.

Wow. I felt a spurt of elation. My powers were growing
so strong!

From his vantage point beside Das Boot, Robbie had
seen it all. He opened the back door without a word, and I
gently placed the box in the backseat. Then he slid smoothly
behind the wheel, I got in, and we drove off. Over my shoulder I watched the little house grow smaller until finally we
went around a bend and it disappeared from sight.

17.
Treasure

January 14, 1999

I am sitting up. Today I ate some broth. Everyone is tip-toeing around me, and Uncle Beck looks at me with a coldness in his eyes the likes of which I've never seen. I keep asking about Linden, but no one will answer. They finally let Athar in today, and I caught her hand and asked her, too, but she just looked at me with those deep, dark eyes. Then they let Alwyn in to see me, but she just sobbed and clutched my hand till they took her away. I realized she's almost fourteen—three months away from her initiation.

Where is Linden? Why has he not come to see me?

Council members have been in and out of the house all week. A net of fear is closing about me. But I dare not name what I fear. It is too horrible.

—Giomanach

"What's in the box?" Robbie asked after a few minutes. He glanced at me. I had cobwebs in my hair, and I was filthy and smelled musty and dirty.

"I don't know," I said. "But it has Maeve's initials on it."

Robbie nodded. "Let's go to my house," he said. "My folks aren't there."

I nodded. "Thanks for driving," I said.

The drive back to Widow's Vale seemed endless. The sun dropped out of the sky shortly after four-thirty, and we drove the last half hour through chilly darkness. I was aching to open the box, but I felt I needed complete security to do it. Robbie parked Das Boot outside his parents' tiny, run-down house. As long as I had known Robbie, they had never repainted their house, or repaired the walk, or done any of the usual homeowner-type stuff. The front lawn was ragged and in need of mowing. It was Robbie's job and he hated it, and his parents didn't seem to care.

I'd never liked coming here, which is why the three of us had usually hung out at Bree's house, our favorite, or my house, our second favorite. Robbie's house was to be avoided, and we all knew it. But for now, it was fine.

Robbie flicked on lights, illuminating the living room, its dingy floor, and the permanent odor of stale cooking and cigarette smoke.

"Where are your folks?" I asked as we walked down the hall to Robbie's room.

"Mom's at her sister's, and Dad's hunting."

"Ugh," I said. "I still remember that time I came over and you had a deer hanging from the tree in your front yard."

Robbie laughed, and we passed through his older sister

Michelle's room. She was away at college, and her room was maintained as a kind of shrine in case she ever came home. Michelle was his parents' favorite, and they made no effort to conceal it. But Robbie didn't resent her. Michelle adored Robbie, and the two of them were very close. I caught a glimpse of a framed school picture of him up on her shelf, taken last year. His face was almost unrecognizable: his skin covered with acne, his eyes concealed by glasses.

Robbie flicked on a lamp. His room was less than half the size of Michelle's, more like a big closet. There was barely enough space for his twin-size bed, which was covered with an old Mexican blanket. A large chest of drawers topped with bookshelves was wedged into a corner. The shelves were overflowing with books, most of them paperbacks, all of them read.

"How's Michelle?" I asked, setting the box carefully on his bed. I was nervous and took my time unbuttoning my coat.

"Fine. She thinks she'll be on the dean's list again."

"Good for her. Is she coming home for Christmas?" My pulse was racing again, but I tried to calm myself. I sat down on the bed.

"Yeah." Robbie grinned. "She's going to be surprised by my looks."

I glanced at him. "Yeah," I said soberly.

"Well, are you gonna open this thing?" he asked, sitting at the other end of his bed.

I swallowed, unwilling to admit how anxious I was. What if there was something awful in there? Something awful or—

"Do you want me to do it?" he asked.

I shook my head quickly. "No—no. I'll do it."

I picked up the box. It was about twenty inches long by sixteen inches wide and about four inches tall. Outside, the metal was flaking off. Two metal clasps held the box shut. They were rusted almost solid. Robbie jumped up and rummaged around in his desk for a screwdriver, then handed it to me. Holding my breath, I wedged it under the lid and pried the clasps free. The lid opened with a pop, and I dug my fingers underneath it and flung it open.

"Wow!" Robbie and I exclaimed at the exact same time.

Though the outside of the box was worn and rusted, the inside of the box was untouched by age or the elements. The interior was shiny and silver. The first thing I saw was an athame. I picked it up. It was heavy in my hand, ancient looking, with an age-worn silver blade and an intricately carved ivory handle. Celtic knots encircled the handle, finely carved but with the unmistakable look of handwork. This hadn't been made in a factory. Turning it over, I saw that the blade itself had been stamped with rows of initials, eighteen pairs of them. The very last ones were M. R. The ones above those were M. R.

"Maeve Riordan," I said, touching the initials. "And Mackenna Riordan, her mother. My grandmother. And me." I felt a rush of happiness. "This came to me from my family." A deep sense of belonging and continuity made me beam with satisfaction. I set the athame carefully on Robbie's bed.

Next I took out a package of deep green silk. When I held it up, it fell into the folds of a robe.

"Cool," said Robbie, touching it gently.

I nodded in agreement, awed. The robe was in the shape

of a large rectangle, with an opening for the head and knots of silk that held the shoulders together.

"It looks like a toga," I said, holding it up to my chest. I blinked, seeing Robbie's questioning face. I smiled at him, knowing that I would try on the robe—but at home, behind locked doors.

The embroidery was astounding: full of Celtic knots, dragons, pentacles, runes, stars, and stylized plants worked in gold and silver thread. It was a work of art, and I could imagine how proud Maeve would have been to inherit it from her mother, to wear it the first time she presided over a circle. As far as I knew, Mackenna had still been high priestess of Belwicket when it was destroyed.

"This is incredible," said Robbie.

"I know," I echoed. "I know."

Folding the robe gently, I laid it aside. Next I found four small silver bowls, embossed again with Celtic symbols. I recognized the runes for air, fire, water, and earth and knew that my birth mother had used these in her circles.

I took out a wand, made of black wood. Thin gold and silver lines had been pounded into the shaft, and the tip was set with a large crystal sphere. Four small red stones circled the wand beneath the crystal, and I wondered if they were real rubies.

Beneath everything, jumbled on the bottom, were several other large chunks of crystal as well as other stones, a feather, and a silver chain with a claddagh charm on it: two hands holding a heart topped with a crown. It was funny: Mom—my adoptive mom—had a claddagh ring that Dad had given her on their twenty-fifth anniversary, last year. The chain felt warm and heavy in my hand.

My gaze swept over all the tools. So much treasure, so much bounty. It was mine: my true inheritance, filled with magick and mystery and power. I felt full of joy but in a way that I could never explain to Robbie . . . in a way I couldn't explain even to myself.

"Two weeks ago I had nothing of my birth mother's," I found myself saying. "Now I have her Book of Shadows and all this besides. I mean, these are things she touched and used. They're full of her magick. And I have them! This is amazing."

Robbie shook his head, his eyes wide. "What's really amazing is that you found out about them by scrying," he murmured.

"I know, I know." Excitement coursed through my veins. "It was like Maeve actually chose to visit me, to give me a message."

"Pretty weird," Robbie acknowledged. "Now, did you say that they didn't do magick while they were in America?"

I nodded. "That's what I've gotten from her Book of Shadows. I mean, I haven't finished reading it yet."

"But she brought all of this with her, anyway? And didn't use it? That must have been really hard."

"Yeah," I said. An inexplicable sense of unease began to cloud my happiness. "I guess she couldn't bear to leave her tools behind, even if she couldn't use them again."

"Maybe she knew she would have a baby," suggested Robbie, "and thought that in time she could pass the tools on. Which she did."

I shrugged. "Could be," I said thoughtfully. "I don't know. Maybe I'll find some explanation in her book."

"I wonder if she thought not using them would protect her somehow," Robbie mused. "Maybe using them would have given away her identity or her location sooner."

I gazed at him, then back at all the stuff. "Maybe so," I said slowly. The unease began to grow. My brows came together as I went on. "Maybe it's still dangerous to have these things. Maybe I shouldn't touch them—or maybe I should put them back."

"I don't know," said Robbie. "Maeve told you where to find them. She didn't seem to be warning you, did she?"

I shook my head. "No. In my vision it felt positive. No warning signs at all." I carefully folded the robe and placed it back in the box, followed by the wand, the athame, and the four small cups. Then I closed the lid. I definitely needed to talk to Cal about this, and also Alyce or David, the next time I saw them.

"So, are you getting together with Cal tonight?" Robbie asked. He grinned. "He's going to flip over all this."

My excitement began to return. "I know. I can't wait to hear what he says about it. Speaking of which, I better go. I have to get cleaned up." I bit my lip, hesitating. "Are you going to Bree's circle tonight?"

"I am," Robbie said easily. He stood and started walking back down the hall. "They're meeting at Raven's."

"Hmmm." I put on my coat and opened the front door, the box tucked securely under my arm. "Well, be careful, okay? And thanks so much for coming with me today. I couldn't have done it without you." I leaned forward and hugged Robbie hard, and he patted my back awkwardly. Then I smiled and waved, and headed out to my car.

My birth mother's tools, I thought as I cranked the engine. I actually had the same tools that had been used by my birth mother, and *her* mother, and her mother's mother, and so on, for possibly hundreds of years . . . if the initials on the athame represented all the high priestesses of Belwicket. I felt a sense of belonging, of family history—one that I knew had somehow been lacking in my life until now. I wished that I could go to Ireland to research their coven and their town and find out what really happened. Maybe someday.

18.
Sigils

January 22, 1999

Now I know. Linden, my brother, barely fifteen years old, is dead. Goddess help me, I am all alone, but for Alwyn. And they say I murdered him.

I look at the words I just wrote, and I cannot make sense of them. Linden is dead. I am accused of Linden's murder.

They say my trial is starting soon. I can't think. My head aches all the time, what I eat my body rejects. I've lost more than two stone and can count my ribs.

My brother is dead.

When I looked at him I saw Mum's face. He is dead, and I am being blamed, though there is no way I would have done it.

—Giomanach

When I got home, no one else was around. I was glad to be by myself; I'd had an idea while I was driving back from Robbie's, and I wanted to test it in private.

First, though, it was time to take some precautions. I got a Phillips-head screwdriver from Dad's toolbox in the mud-room. Then I carried the box with Maeve's tools up to the second-floor landing. Unscrewing the HVAC vent cover, I pulled it out from the wall and set the box inside the vent. When I screwed the cover back on, it would be totally invisible. I knew because I'd used this spot as a hiding place over the years—I'd kept my first diary here, and Mary K.'s favorite doll when I hid it from her after a huge fight.

Before I closed the vent, though, I took out the athame, the beautiful, antique athame with my mother's initials on it. I loved the fact that my initials were the same as hers and my grandmother's. I ran my fingers gently over the carved handle as I carried the athame downstairs.

About a week before, I'd been looking for information about Wicca on-line, and I'd come across an old article by a woman named Helen Firesdaughter. It described the traditional witch's tools and their uses. The athame, the article had said, was linked with the element of fire. It was used to direct energy and to symbolize and bring about change. It was also used to illuminate, to bring hidden things to light.

I pulled on my coat, then stepped outside into the frigid dusk and closed the front door behind me. A quick glance up and down the street assured me that no one was watching. Holding the athame in front of me like a metal detector, I began to walk around my house. I swept the ancient blade over windowsills, doors, the clapboard siding, whatever I could reach.

I found the first sigil on the porch railing, around to the side. To the naked eye there was nothing there, but when the athame swept over it, the rune glowed very faintly, with an ethereal bluish witch light. My throat tightened. So— there it was. Proof that Sky and Hunter had worked magick here last night. I traced its lines and curves with my finger. Peorth. It stood for hidden things revealed.

I breathed deeply, trying to stay calm and rational. Peorth. Well, that didn't tell me much about their plans, one way or the other. I'd have to keep looking.

As I circled the house, more and more sigils glowed under the athame's blade. Daeg, for awakening and clarity. Eoh, the horse, which means change of some kind. Othel, for birthright, inheritance. And then, on the clapboards directly below my bedroom window, I found the one I'd been dreading to see: the double fishhook of Yr.

I stared at it and felt like a fist was squeezing my lungs. Yr. The death rune. Cal had told me that it didn't always have to mean death—that it could mean some other kind of important ending. I tried to take comfort in that possibility. But I was having a hard time convincing myself.

Then I felt a tingle at the edge of my senses. Someone was nearby. Watching me.

I spun around, peering into the dim winter twilight. A lone street lamp cast a cone of yellow light outside our yard. But I could see no shadowed form, no flicker of movement anywhere, not even when I used my magesight. Nor could I feel the presence any longer. Was I imagining it? Sensing things that weren't really there?

I didn't know. All I knew was that suddenly I couldn't

bear to be outside, alone, for one second longer. Turning, I bolted into the house and locked the door behind me.

By the time Cal came to pick me up, I had calmed down enough that I was feeling excited about my special birthday celebration.

"What's changed about you?" Cal asked as I pulled the front door closed. He smiled at me, puzzled. "You look different. Your eyes are different."

I batted my lashes at him. "I'm wearing makeup," I said. "Mary K. finally got her mitts on me. I figured, why not? It's a special occasion."

He laughed and took my arm, and together we walked to his car. "Well, you look incredible, but don't think you have to wear it on my account." He opened my door and then went around to the driver's side.

"Did you get my messages?" I asked as he started the engine.

He nodded. "Mom said you called." He didn't mention the witch message. "Sorry I missed you. I had some errands to do." He wiggled his eyebrows at me. "Mysterious errands, if you know what I mean, Birthday Girl."

I smiled briefly, but I was impatient to tell him about the events of the last 24 hours. "I had a pretty eventful day without you. In fact, I've had *two* pretty eventful days." I hunkered lower in my coat.

"What happened?" he asked.

I opened my mouth, and before I knew it, everything was tumbling out of me like an avalanche: the headlights behind me that had made me wreck, scrying into the fire, seeing Sky and Hunter outside my house the night before. Cal kept shooting glances at me, some baffled, some shocked, some worried. Then I offered up my pièce de résistance, finding Maeve's tools.

"You found your mother's tools?" he cried. The car swerved. I wondered for a second if it was going to end up like Das Boot. Luckily, though, we were turning into his driveway.

I threw up my hands and grinned. "I can't believe it myself," I said.

He cut the engine and sat there, staring at me in amazement. "Did you bring them?" he asked eagerly.

"No," I admitted. "I hid them behind the HVAC vent. And then when I was leaving, Dad was fixing an electrical outlet in the hall and I couldn't get to them."

Cal gave me an amused, conspiratorial look. "Behind the HVAC vent," he repeated, and I couldn't help laughing with him. It was a pretty silly hiding place for a bunch of magickal tools, come to think of it.

"Oh, well, no big deal. You can show them to me tomorrow," he said. I nodded.

"So—what do you think about my accident?" I asked.

"I don't know," he murmured. He shook his head. "It could have been just some jerk who was in a hurry. But if you were scared, I say you should trust your instincts—and we should start asking some questions." His eyes seemed to harden, but then his face melted in a worried smile. "Why didn't you tell me about this last night? And about Hunter and Sky being at your house?"

"I sent you a witch message," I told him. "But you

never came. I was wondering if Sky could have blocked it somehow."

Cal frowned. Then he smacked his forehead. "No, that's not it. I know exactly what it was. Mom and I did a powerful warding spell before our circle, just in case people like Sky or Hunter were trying to snoop on us. That would have blocked your message. Wow, I am so sorry. It never occurred to me that you might try to reach me."

"It's okay," I told him. "Nothing happened to me." A shudder ran through me as I remembered my terror last night. "At least, nothing permanent."

We got out of the car, shivering, and hurried up his front steps together.

We met Selene on her way out. She was wrapped in a black velvet cloak that swept to the ground and wore shining purple amethysts around her neck and on her ears. As always, she looked stunning.

"Good evening, my dears," she said with a smile. A delicious scent wafted off her, giving me an impression of maturity, of richness. It made my own dab of patchouli oil seem naive and hippyish—girly, almost.

"You look beautiful," I said sincerely.

"Thank you, Birthday Girl. So do you," she said, pulling on black gloves. "I'm going to a party." She shot Cal a meaningful look. "I won't be back till quite late, so be on your best behavior."

I felt embarrassed, but Cal laughed easily. As Selene left through the wide front door, we started to climb the stairs to his room on the third floor.

"Um, what does your mom think we might do?" I asked

clumsily. My steps were muffled by the thick carpet on the stairs.

"I guess she thinks we might make love," Cal said. Judging from his tone, it sounded like he was talking about spending the evening playing board games. He flashed a casual smile.

I nearly fell down the stairs. "Uh—would she . . . you know, be upset?" I stammered, struggling to sound calm but failing miserably. All of my friends' parents would have a cow if they thought their kids were doing that under their own roof. Well, maybe not Jenna's. But everyone else's.

"No," said Cal. "In Wicca, making love doesn't have the same kind of stigma as it does in other religions. It's seen as a celebration of love, of life—an acknowledgment of the God and Goddess. It's beautiful. Something special."

"Oh." Blood pounded through me. I nodded, trying to look confident.

Cal closed the door behind him. Then he pulled me to him and kissed me. "I'm sorry I wasn't there for you last night," he breathed against my lips. "I know I've been really tied up with Mom's business lately. But from now on I'm going to make sure I'm more available."

I reached up and draped my arms around his neck. "Good," I said.

He held me for a moment longer, then gently disengaged my arms and grabbed some matches from the nightstand by his bed. As I watched, he lit candles around his room, one by one, until there were tiny flames everywhere. The candles lined the mantel, the top of every bookcase, stood in holders on the floor; there was even an old-fashioned iron chandelier that held candles, hanging from the ceiling. When he turned off the overhead light, we found ourselves surrounded in a glowing fiery cocoon. It was dreamy, beautiful, romantic.

Next Cal walked over to his dark wooden desk, where a bottle of sparkling cider stood next to a bowl filled with perfect, amazingly red strawberries and another bowl of dipping chocolate. He poured two glasses of cider and brought me one.

"Thank you," I said happily. "This is incredible." The light, golden cider tickled my throat with its starry little bubbles.

He came and sat down next to me again, and we drank our cider. "I can't wait to see Maeve's tools," he said, stroking the hair along my temple. "The historical value alone—it's like finding King Tut's tomb."

I laughed. "The Wiccan version of King Tut's tomb. Which reminds me. I kept one thing out, and brought it with me." Putting my glass down on the nightstand, I hopped up and went to my jacket, where I took out the athame from the breast pocket. I had wrapped it in a handkerchief. Silently I handed it to Cal, watching his face as I nestled back down with him again.

"Goddess," he whispered as he unwrapped it. His eyes were shining, and an eager smile played about his lips. "Oh, Morgan, this is beautiful."

I laughed again at his excitement. "I know. Isn't it amazing?"

His fingers traced the lines of initials carved into the blade. "Tomorrow," he said absently, then looked up at me. "Tomorrow," he said more firmly, "I'm going to have a busy day. First I have to find Hunter and Sky and tell them to leave you the hell alone. Then I have to go to your house and remove all their sigils, if I can. Then I have to salivate over your mother's tools."

"Oh, that's a lovely image," I said, laughing. "Thank you."

He laughed, too, then we were leaning together, kissing and sipping cider. Magick, I thought dreamily, staring at him.

Cal kissed me again, his golden eyes intent, and then he blinked and pulled back.

"Presents!" he said, motioning across the room.

It took a second to spot the pile of beautifully wrapped gifts that waited for me on a large table pushed against the wall.

"What have you done?" I asked, putting my hand to my throat, where his silver pentacle still nestled warm against my skin. It was the first thing he'd ever given me, and I treasured it for that.

He grinned and stood, carrying the presents back to the bed and spreading them before me on the mattress. I took another sip of my cider, then placed it on the nightstand again.

First was a rectangular box. I started pulling off the paper.

"This is kind of redundant now," he said.

My face melted in a smile. Inside the box was the silver athame we had seen at Practical Magick, the one carved with roses and a skull. I turned to him.

"It's lovely," I said, running my fingers across it.

"It can be your backup," he said cheerfully. "Or a cake knife. Or a letter opener."

"Thank you," I whispered.

"I wanted you to have it," Cal said. "Next."

He held out a small box, and I held my breath as I opened it, revealing a gorgeous pair of silver earrings set with golden tigereyes. The gems looked so much like Cal's eyes that I had to glance up at him just for the sake of comparison.

"These are so beautiful." I shook my head.

"Put them on," he encouraged, "and it will be like I'm always with you." He brushed back my hair to expose my earlobe.

I held the earrings, not knowing what to say.

"Your ears aren't pierced," Cal said in surprise.

"I know," I mumbled apologetically. "My mom took me and Bree to have it done when we were twelve, but I chickened out."

"Oh, Morgan, I'm sorry," he said, laughing. "It's my fault. I can't believe I didn't notice before now. I should have gotten you something else. Here—I'll take them back and exchange them."

"No!" I said, pulling the box close. "I love them—they're the most beautiful things I've ever seen. I've been wanting to get my ears pierced, anyway. This will be my inspiration."

Cal looked at me assessingly but appeared to take my word. "Hmmm. Well, okay." He nodded at another present.

Next was a beautifully bound and illustrated book about spell weaving. It included a short history of spell making and had a whole section of sample spells and how to use them as well as how to individualize them for your particular situation.

"Oh, this is fabulous," I said with enthusiasm, leafing through it. "This is perfect."

"I'm glad you like it," he said, grinning. "We can go over some of them if you want, practice them."

I nodded eagerly, like a child, and he laughed again.

"And last," he said, handing me a medium-size box.

"More?" I couldn't quite believe this. I was beginning to feel spoiled. Inside this box was a batik blouse in muted shades of lavender and purple and plum. It looked like a storm-shot sunset. I stared at it, touching the cloth with my fingers, drinking in the colors, practically hearing the rumble of thunder and rain.

"I love it," I said, leaning over to hug him. "I love all of it. Thank you so much for this." My throat tightened with a rush of emotion. Once again I felt a sense of belonging, of pure contentment. "These are the best birthday gifts anyone has ever given me."

Cal gave me a sweet smile, and then I was in his arms and we were lying on the bed. I held his head tightly, my fingers laced through his dark hair as we kissed.

"Do you love me?" he whispered against my mouth. I nodded, overwhelmed, holding him hard against me, wanting to be closer.

The cider, the candles all around us, the slight scent of incense, the feel of his smooth skin under my hands—it was as if he were weaving a spell of love around me, making me drowsy and full of a physical longing and ache. And yet . . . and yet. I still held the end of a line between us. Despite my love for him, despite the dark wave of yearning he had awoken in me, I felt myself holding back.

Dimly, as we kissed, I came to the surprising realization that I wasn't quite ready to completely give myself to him. Even though we were probably *mùirn beatha dàns,* still, I wasn't ready to make love with him, to go all the way in joining ourselves together physically and mentally. I didn't know the reason, but I had to trust my feelings.

"Morgan," Cal said softly. He raised up on one elbow and looked at me. He was incredibly beautiful, the most beautiful male I had ever seen. His cheeks were flushed, his mouth a dark rose color from kissing. There was no way he and Hunter could be brothers, I thought distantly—and I wondered why Hunter had even popped into my thoughts. Hunter was mean and dangerous, a liar.

"Come on," Cal said, his voice husky, his hand stroking my waist through my black jumper.

"Um . . ."

"What's wrong?" he whispered.

I let out my breath, not knowing what to say. He draped one leg over me and pulled me closer, curling his hand around my back and snuggling. He nuzzled my neck, and his hand drifted up my waist to just below my breast. It felt incredible, and I willed myself to give in to it, to let the wash of sensation carry me to a new place. I would be seventeen tomorrow: it was time. But somehow I just couldn't. . . .

"Morgan?" His voice sounded questioning, and my eyes flew to his. His hand stroked my hair away from my face. "I want to make love to you."

19.
Circle of Two

They are pushing me to join with her. And I want to do it. Goddess, how I want to do it. She is a butterfly, a flower in bloom, a dark ruby being cut from dusty stone. And I can make her better than that. I can make her catch fire, so her power illuminates all who stand near. I can teach her, I can help her reach the deep magick within. Together we will be unstoppable.

Whoever would have thought this could happen? One look at her would not have revealed the tigress waiting inside. Her love devours me, her constancy humbles me, her beauty and power make me hunger.

She will be mine. And I will be hers.

— Sgàth

I stared at Cal, loving him but feeling utterly lost.

"I thought you wanted me, too," he said quietly.

I nodded. That was true—partially, anyway. But what my brain wanted and my body wanted were two different things.

"If you're worried about birth control, I can take care of it," he said. "I wouldn't ever hurt you."

"I know." I could feel tears welling up in my eyes, and I willed them to stop. I felt like a complete failure, and I didn't know why.

Cal rolled away from me, his arm resting across his forehead as he looked at me. "So what is it?" he said.

"I don't know," I whispered. "I mean, I want to, but I just can't. I don't feel ready."

He reached out his other hand and held mine, absently stroking his thumb across my palm. Finally he shifted and sat up cross-legged in front of me. I scrambled into a sitting position opposite him.

"Are you angry?" I asked.

He smiled wryly. "I'll live. It's okay. Don't worry about it. I . . ." He left the sentence unfinished.

"I'm sorry," I said miserably. "I don't know what's wrong with me."

He leaned over and pushed my hair off my neck to kiss my nape gently. I shuddered at the warmth of his lips. "Nothing is wrong with you," he whispered. "We have our whole future together. There's no hurry. Whenever you're ready, I'll be here."

I swallowed, worrying that if I opened my mouth again, I would definitely start crying.

"Look, let's do a circle," he said, rubbing the tension out of my neck. "Not a *circle* circle, but just like a joined meditation. It's another way for us to be close. Okay?"

I nodded. "Okay," I choked out.

I reached for him, and we held hands loosely, with our knees touching. Together we closed our eyes and began to systematically shut everything down: emotions, sensations, awareness of the outside world. I felt embarrassed about not wanting to sleep with him, but I deliberately released those feelings. It was almost as if I could see them falling away from me. My eyes stopped stinging; my throat relaxed.

Gradually our breathing, in sync, slowed and quieted. I had been meditating almost every day, and it was easy for me to slip into a light trance. I lost the sensation of touching Cal: we felt joined, breathing as one, drifting as one into a place of deep peace and restfulness. It was a relief.

I became aware of the strength of Cal's mind, aligning with mine, and it was very exciting and intimate. It was amazing that we could share this, and I thought of all the nonwitches in the world who would probably never be able to achieve such closeness with their lovers. I breathed a long sigh of contentment.

In our meditation I felt Cal's thoughts; I read the intensity of his passion, felt his desire for me, and my flesh broke out in goosebumps. I felt his admiration of my strength in the craft, as well as eagerness for me to progress—to get stronger and stronger, as strong as he was. I tried to share my own thoughts with him, unsure if he was reading me as well. I expressed my desires and hopes for our future together; I tried to let waves of pure emotion convey my feelings in a way that words never could.

Eventually we drifted apart, like two leaves separating as they fell toward earth. I slipped back into my self, and we remained there for a while afterward, gazing at each other. It was the most intensely connected I had ever felt to another person. I knew it. But knowing this also made me feel vulnerable and nervous.

"Was it good for you?" I asked, trying to lighten the moment.

He smiled. "It was great for me."

I looked into his face for a while longer, allowing myself to get lost in his eyes, enjoying the silence and the glow of the candles. Dimly I became aware of the ticking of a clock nearby. I glanced at it.

"Oh my God, is it one o'clock?" I gasped.

Cal looked, too, and grinned. "Hmmm. Do you have a curfew?"

I was already climbing off the bed. "Not officially," I said, searching for my shoes. "But I'm supposed to call if I'm later than midnight. Of course, if I call now, I'll wake them up." Quickly I gathered my presents into a pile. I found Maeve's athame and put it back inside my coat. We trotted downstairs. A pang of longing welled up inside me; I wanted to stay *here,* in the warmth and coziness of Cal's room, with him.

Cold wind blasted my face when we stepped through the front door.

"Ugh," I moaned, gripping the neck of my coat tighter.

Heads down, we hurried out to Cal's Explorer. "Maybe we should call your folks and tell them you're having a sleepover," he suggested with a grin.

I laughed, thinking of how well that would go over with Mom and Dad, then carefully placed my beautiful birthday presents on the backseat. But as I was about to climb into the front, the sound of a car arriving made me pause. I glanced at Cal. His eyes had narrowed. He looked alert and tense, his hand on the car door next to me.

"Is it your mom?" I asked.

Cal shook his head. "That's not her car."

Using magesight, I squinted into the approaching headlights, staring right past them. My heart lurched. It was a gray car. Hunter's car.

He pulled to a stop in front of us.

"Oh God, what's he doing here?" I groaned. "It's one in the morning!"

"Who knows?" Cal said tersely. "But I need to talk to him, anyway."

Hunter left his car running as he stepped out and faced us. The headlights put him in silhouette, but I could see that his green eyes were solemn. His cold seemed to have gotten better. His breath was like white smoke.

"Hello," he said precisely. Just hearing him speak made me clench up. "Fancy meeting the both of you here. How inconvenient."

"Why?" Cal asked, his voice low. "Were you going to put sigils on my house, like you did Morgan's?"

A glimmer of surprise crossed Hunter's face.

"Know about that, do you?" he said, shifting his gaze to me.

I nodded coldly.

"What else do you know?" Hunter asked. "Like, do you know what Cal wants from you? What you are to him? Do you know the truth about *anything*?"

I glared at him, trying to think of a scathing reply. But

again the only thought I had was: Why is he tormenting us like this?

Beside me Cal clenched his fists. "She knows the truth. I love her."

"No," Hunter corrected him. "The truth is, you *need* her. You need her because she has incredible, untapped powers. You need her so you can use her power to take over the High Council, and then you can start to eliminate the other clans, one by one. Because you're a Woodbane, too, and frankly, the other clans just aren't good enough."

My eyes flashed to Cal. "What is he talking about? You're not a Woodbane, are you?"

"He's raving," Cal muttered, staring at Hunter with pure contempt. "Saying anything he can think of to hurt me." Cal put his arm around me. "You can forget breaking us up," he said. "She loves me, and I love her."

Hunter laughed. The sound of it was like glass shattering. "What a crock," he spat. "She's your lightning rod—the last surviving member of Belwicket, the destined high priestess of one of the most powerful of the Woodbane clans. Don't you get it? Belwicket renounced the dark arts! There's no way Morgan would agree to what you want!"

"How would *you* know what I would do?" I shouted, infuriated by how he was speaking as if I weren't there.

Cal just shook his head. "There's no point to this," he said. "We're together, and there's nothing you can do. So you can go back to where you came from and leave us alone."

Hunter chuckled softly. "Oh, no, I'm afraid it's much too late for that. You see, the council would never forgive me if I left Morgan in your clutches."

"What?" I practically screeched. What the hell did the council care who I dated? I hardly even *knew* about the council. How could they know so much about me?

"You should know about forgiveness," Cal snapped. "After all, the council has never quite forgiven you for killing your brother, right? You're still making up for that, aren't you? Still trying to prove it wasn't your fault."

I stared at the two of them. I had no idea what Cal was talking about, but his tone terrified me. He sounded like a stranger.

"Go to hell," Hunter snarled, his body tightening.

"Wiccans don't believe in hell," Cal whispered.

Hunter started toward us, his face stiff with fury. All at once Cal ducked into the car and snatched the athame he'd given me from the pile of gifts. My pulse shot into overdrive. This isn't happening, I thought in panic. This can't be happening. I watched, immobile, as Cal backed away from me. Hunter glanced between the two of us.

"You want me?" Cal taunted Hunter. "You want me, Hunter? Then come get me." With that, he turned and sped straight for the dark woods bordering the property. I blinked, and he was out of sight, hidden by trees and darkness.

Hunter was wild-eyed as he scanned the woods' edge.

"Stay here!" he commanded me, then he raced off after Cal.

I stopped for just a moment. Then I ran after them.

20.
The Seeker

February 12, 1999

With help, now, I can walk across a room. But I am still weak, so weak.

My trial is starting tomorrow.

I have been telling my story over and over, what I remember of it. I woke in the night and saw Linden was gone. I tracked him to the fell, and found him in the middle of calling a <u>taibhs</u>, a dark spirit. It is something we had talked about in the past year, in our search for answers about our parents. But I had not counseled Linden to do it, nor would I have ever condoned his trying to summon the evil thing alone.

I saw Linden, his arms upstretched, a look of joy on his face. The dark taibhs moved toward him, and I rushed forward. I could not get through the circle without magick so I conjured a break in the force. The rest of what I remember is a nightmare of reaching for Linden, of finding him and having him sag in my arms, of being surrounded by a choking wraith, then being smothered, unable to breathe, and sinking down to the cold ground to embrace death.

Next I woke in my bed at Uncle Beck and Aunt Shelagh's, with witches around me praying for my recovery, after six days of unconsciousness.

I know I did not kill my brother, but I know that my quest to redress the harm done my family is what caused his death. For this I could be sentenced to death. Except that I know Alwyn would grieve for me, I would welcome it, for there is no life for me here anymore.

—Giomanach

By the time I reached the edge of the woods, it had started to snow again. While Cal and I were inside, the sky had been consumed by thick gray clouds that blotted out the moon and the stars.

"Dammit," I whispered. Cal had obviously led Hunter away to protect me, but how could he expect me to stand around, waiting to see what happened? I didn't know what was going on between the two of them. All I knew was that I would never forgive Hunter if he hurt Cal.

The woods were dense and untamed, the undergrowth thick and impossible to run through. I ran into a low-hanging branch, and I stopped. I had no idea where Cal and Hunter had gone. It was absolutely black here, and for a moment I trembled. I had to breathe slowly, to focus and concentrate. I clenched and unclenched my fists and squeezed my eyes shut.

"One, two, three," I counted. I breathed in and out.

A moment later I opened my eyes and found that my magesight had kicked in and I could see. Trees stood out as dark verticals, the undergrowth was defined, and the few nocturnal animals and birds who weren't hibernating glowed with a pale yellow light. Okay. I scanned the area, and easily picked up the rough track Hunter and Cal had made as they crashed through the woods: the forest floor was scraped and disturbed, and small branches were snapped.

As quickly as I could, I followed their trail. My feet and nose were freezing, and snow began to fall and bleach the surroundings. Slowly I became aware of a dim, rhythmic pounding. It wasn't the blood in my veins. Then it came to me: of course. Selene and Cal lived at the edge of town; their house was practically on the Hudson River. The surging waters were dead ahead. I quickened my pace, grabbing trees to push me forward, stumbling against rocks, cursing.

"You're bidden to come with me!"

It was Hunter's voice. I stopped silent, listening—then rushed forward and came out into a narrow, treeless strip that ran parallel with the river. Hunter was backed against the edge of the cliff, and Cal, holding my athame in front of him, was moving forward. I was lost in a swirl of fear and confusion.

"Cal!" I shouted.

They both turned, their faces unreadable in the snow and darkness.

"Stay back!" Cal ordered me, flinging out his hand. To my utter shock I stopped hard, as if I'd struck a wall. He had used a spell against me.

The next instant Hunter hurled a ball of witch light, and it knocked the athame from Cal's hand. Cal's jaw dropped. I struggled to believe that this was real, my real life, and not just a screen full of computer-generated effects. Hunter leaped away from the edge and onto Cal, who was scrambling back toward the knife. As I tried to move forward, I felt like I was wrapped in a thick wool blanket. My legs were made of stone. The two of them rolled over in the new-fallen snow, light hair and dark flashing against the ground and the background of night.

"Stop it!" I shouted as loud as I could, but they ignored me.

Cal pinned Hunter on the ground, then closed his fist and smashed it into Hunter's face. Hunter's head whipped sideways. A bright ribbon of blood streamed from his nose. The redness on the snow reminded me of the spilled communion wine last Sunday, and I shuddered. This was wrong. This shouldn't be happening. This kind of anger, of long-held hatred, was the antithesis of magick. I had to separate them.

Gathering all my strength, I pictured myself breaking out of an eggshell and then tried to shove my way out of Cal's binding spell. This time I was able to move. A few feet away I saw the athame, and I lunged for it—at the very moment Hunter shoved Cal off him. We all stumbled to our feet at the same time, panting heavily.

"Morgan, get out of here!" Hunter yelled at me, not taking his eyes off Cal. "I'm a Seeker, and Cal has to answer to the council!"

"Don't listen to him, Morgan!" Cal retorted. I saw flecks of Hunter's blood on his fist. "He's jealous of anything I have, and he wants to hurt me. He'll hurt you, too!"

"That's a lie," Hunter spat angrily. "Cal's Woodbane, Morgan, but unlike Maeve, he hasn't renounced the dark side. Please, just get out of here!"

Cal turned to me, and his hot golden eyes caught mine. A fuzzy softness clouded my brain. I blinked. Hunter said something, but it was muffled, and time seemed to slow. What was happening to me? I watched helplessly as Hunter and Cal circled each other, their eyes burning, their faces stony and pale.

Hunter spoke again, waving his arm, and it fluttered through the air slowly. His voice was like the deep growl of an animal. They came softly together—as if their movements were choreographed—and Hunter's fist connected with Cal's stomach. Cal doubled over. I winced, but I was trapped in a nightmare, powerless to stop the fight. I clutched the athame to my chest. There was a small knot of heat at my throat. I touched the warm silver of the pentacle hanging there. But I couldn't move toward them.

Cal straightened. Hunter swung again at him but missed. Then Cal kicked the back of Hunter's knee, and Hunter crumpled to the ground, the blood on his face smearing the snow. Memories flashed through my mind as Hunter staggered to his feet and threw himself on Cal . . . Hunter telling me Cal was Woodbane, Hunter in the dark outside my house, Hunter being so snide and hateful.

I remembered Cal kissing me, touching me, showing me magick. Showing me how to ground myself at circles, giving me presents. I thought of Bree yelling at me in her car by the side of the road, so long ago. Sky and Hunter together. The images made me unbearably weary. All I wanted to do was lie down in the snow and fall asleep. I sank to my knees, feeling a smile form on my lips. Sleep, I thought. There must have been magick at work, but it didn't seem to matter.

In front of me Cal and Hunter rolled over and over, toward the river.

"Morgan."

My name came to me softly, on a snowflake, and I looked up. For just an instant I met Cal's eyes. They stared pleadingly at me. Then I saw that Hunter was holding Cal down, his knee on Cal's chest. He had a length of silver chain and was binding Cal's hands with it while Cal writhed in pain.

"Morgan."

I received a sharp flash of his pain. I gasped and grabbed my chest, falling forward onto the snow. As I blinked rapidly, my head suddenly seemed clearer.

"He's killing me. Help me. Morgan!"

I couldn't hear the words, but I felt them inside my head, and I pushed myself to my feet with one hand.

"You're through," Hunter was gasping angrily, pulling the silver chain. "I've got you."

"Morgan!" Cal's shout ripped through the snowy night and shattered my calm. I had to move, to fight. I loved Cal, had always loved him. I struggled to my feet as if I had been asleep for a long, long time. I had no plan; I was no match for Hunter, but suddenly I remembered I was still clutching the athame, my birthday athame. Without thinking, I hurled it at Hunter as hard as I could. I watched as it sailed through the air in a gleaming arc.

It struck Hunter's neck, quivering there for a second before falling. Hunter cried out and clapped his hand to the wound. Blood began to spout from the flesh, blooming red like a poppy. I couldn't believe what I had done.

In that second Cal drew up his knees and kicked Hunter as hard as he could. With a cry of surprise Hunter staggered back, off balance, still clutching his wound . . . and then I was screaming, "No! No! No!" as he toppled clumsily and disappeared over the edge of the cliff.

I stared at the emptiness, dumbstruck.

"Morgan, help!" Cal cried, startling me. "Get this off! It's burning me! Get it off!"

Numb, I hurried to Cal and pulled at the silver chain looped around his wrists. I felt nothing but a mild tingle when I touched it—but I saw raw, red blistering welts on Cal's skin where it had touched him. Once it was off, I threw down the chain and scrambled to the edge of the cliff. If I saw Hunter's body at the bottom, on the rocks, I knew I would throw up, but I forced myself to look, already thinking about calling 911, about trying to climb down there, wondering if I remembered CPR from my baby-sitting course.

But I saw nothing. Nothing but a jumble of rocks and the gray, turbulent water.

Cal staggered up beside me. I met his eyes. He looked horrified, pale and hollow and weak. "Goddess, he's already gone," Cal murmured. "He must have hit the water, and the current . . ." He was breathing hard, his dark hair wet with snow and traces of blood.

"We have to call someone," I said softly, reaching out to touch him. "We have to tell someone about Hunter. And we have to take care of your wrists. Do you think you can get back to the house?"

Cal just shook his head. "Morgan," he said in a broken voice. "You saved me." With fingers swollen from hitting Hunter, he touched my cheek and said tenderly, "You saved me. Hunter was going to kill me, but you protected me from him, like you said you would. I love you." He kissed me, his lips cold and tasting of blood. "I love you more than I ever knew I could. Today our future truly begins."

I didn't know what to say. My thoughts had stopped swirling; they had vanished altogether. My mind was a void. I put my arm around him as he began to limp back through the woods, and I couldn't help glancing over my shoulder to the cliff's edge. It was all too much to take in, everything that had happened, and I concentrated on putting one foot in front of the other, feeling Cal rest some of his weight on me as we slogged through the snow.

And then I remembered: it was November 23.

I wondered what time it was—I knew it was very late. I had been born at two-seventeen in the morning on November 23. I decided I must already be officially seventeen. I swallowed. This was the first day of my seventeenth year. What would tomorrow bring?